The Green-Coated Boy

The Green-Coated Boy

by

MARJORIE DIXON

and

RICHARD KENNEDY

illustrated by

RICHARD KENNEDY

A Wonderful World Book

A. S. BARNES AND COMPANY, INC.

New York

© 1957 by Marjorie Dixon and Richard Kennedy

Published in the United States by
A. S. Barnes and Company, Inc. 1959

Library of Congress Catalog Card Number: 59-12804

Printed in the United States of America

For
CRISPIAN
and
ROBERT

Acknowledgments

My acknowledgments and thanks are due to the firm of Messrs. Ernest Benn, publishers of the late Dr. Douglas Hyde's *Literary History of Ireland* for their kind permission to use his beautiful translation of the poem *Midir's Call to Fairyland*. But it is with deep regret that I have to state that all efforts I have made to get in touch with the family and literary executors of Dr. Hyde himself have been in vain.

M.D.

Contents

CHAPTER I

Ulphin

"Where is this place, Ulphin?" asked Josephine. "Is it on the mountain?"

"No," said Dominic.

"Is it in the fields?"

"No."

"Is it a house?"

"No!" And Dominic shut his mouth firmly, enjoying tantalizing his sister's curiosity.

"Get on with your tea," said Nellie, pushing the soda bread towards them with a plump red arm. "I have the chickens to feed."

Dominic and Josephine were twins. And although they were not identical twins they still contrived to be so much alike that if you dressed Josephine, as she sometimes chose to do herself, in shorts and a shirt and cut her hair off, as she threatened to do each time that Nellie washed it in ammonia, she and Dominic would look like one little boy and his reflection in the looking-glass. And if, contrariwise, you put Dominic into a red cotton dress like the one Josephine was wearing, and left him in it till his hair had grown a little longer, the two of them would almost look like the same little girl; almost but not quite, for in the first case you would notice that one of the two little boys had a gentler, calmer look, as though he had come to accept the world as it is and make the best of it; and in the other you would think what a wild little rebel it was that had got into the skin of a girl.

The children, who were eleven years old, lived with their Uncle Theo in that part of Ireland through which the Shan-

non flows—the longest river in the British Isles, and where Slieve Aneurin, the nearest and handsomest of the surrounding mountains, stands like a guardian watching over its slender beginnings. The three of them and Nellie, who looked after them all, lived in a big grey square house like a match-box, with an old rusty bell on the wall that dated back to the eighteenth century. It was known as the Rectory and had huge cellars beneath it into which the children had never penetrated. They did not see much of their uncle, who spent most of his time studying ancient Irish texts. Nellie mended their clothes, all of which dated back to the time a year and a half ago when their parents had left them, to return to the Gold Coast. Since Dominic had had that trouble with his glands, they had decided that the Gold Coast was not the best place in the world for children, and so the twins were left at the Rectory with injunctions that they were to be good children, do everything that their uncle told them, and never on any account drink anything but goat's milk. And their parents had bought them for their very own a beautiful little white nanny goat with long horns and a pedigree even longer. Amalthea was the name their uncle had given her, saying it was the name of a goat that had brought up a god, and he hoped that this one would be as lucky and then he would count himself lucky too. This afternoon it was Dominic's turn to fetch Amalthea home from the patch of waste land next door to Miss Morrissey's. The children liked making this journey because Miss Morrissey, who kept the little shop opposite John O'Connell's, sometimes called them in and gave them a ginger biscuit or a chocolate cream bar. It was after Dominic had shared his chocolate cream bar with Josephine and sat down to his tea that this word Ulphin had first come into the conversation, and now that Nellie had left the room, Josephine tilted her chair forwards and fixed her eyes expectantly on her twin, knowing well that Dominic could not possibly resist a listener as sympathetic as she believed herself to be.

Dominic avoided her eyes once or twice and she was careful to utter no word to break the silence that he seemed bent on keeping. At last, "Was it at Miss Morrissey's," she ventured to help him out, "that they told you about Ulphin?"

"It was not," Dominic answered quite readily, as though

he had only been waiting to make up his mind how to begin. "But it was whilst I was standing at her gate taking out the grass that had got caught in the goat's chain that I noticed a man with a fiddle talking to a lot of chaps outside John O'Connell's. He saw me too, and after a bit he called out something about Amalthea being a beautiful little goat."

Josephine nodded, for both children adored their goat who was, in a sense, the only thing they had of their very own.

"So I crossed over to John O'Connell's," Dominic continued, "and showed Amalthea off to him and he kept on saying what a womanish sort of face she had, and what a sleek wedge shape was her body, until at last I said, 'You seem to know an awful lot about goats.' But he only laughed."

Josephine nodded again. "What was he like?" she asked.

"Oh, quite young." Dominic paused. "You know that picture in Uncle Theo's study? It's of a man with a face that's somehow twisted, as though something had gone wrong with him."

"I know," said Josephine brightening. "His name is John Keats. It's written underneath. He looks as though he had toothache or something, but didn't really mind that as much as something else."

"Well, he was rather like that picture, and I saw he was lame, because there was a crutch leaning on the wall outside John O'Connell's. The other men seemed to know who he was, because some of them were calling him Miley. Then he started playing his fiddle. He played it far better than any one you'd hear about here—or perhaps it was just the tune that was different from anything else . . ." Dominic broke off, puckering his forehead.

"Did it make you want to dance?" Josephine suggested.

"No, it wasn't a dance tune."

"Did it make you want to laugh?" his sister tried.

"No, it wasn't that kind of a tune either."

"Then it must have made you want to cry," said Josephine with finality. "But what had it got to do with Ulphin?"

"Of course it didn't make me want to cry," Dominic

answered very crossly. "And if you say such silly things, I shan't tell you about Ulphin."

And he turned his back to her and went over to the window. But after a few moments and with his back still towards her he presently went on talking, and this time his voice sounded different; almost dreamy.

"At last he stopped playing and I asked him what was the name of the tune?"

"And he said it was Ulphin," Josephine breathed, her voice beginning to be tinged with awe.

This time Dominic was not cross. "No, that comes later. The name of the tune, he said, was *The Green-coated Boy*. But it had never been written down, for he'd heard it from Michael the Drover, and he had it from the Boy himself."

"And *his* name was Ulphin!" Josephine cried, sure now that she had got it at last.

"No it wasn't, silly. And don't keep interrupting. This is what Miley told me about him. He said that he's as beautiful as an archangel, and he lives on a mountain top and herds a flock of pure-bred goats, and he plays on the Irish pipes. It seems that Black Michael—that's what he called the drover, and he had a great shock of black hair—one day Black Michael met two friends of his on a mountain where they had a still."

"What's that?" Josephine wanted to know.

"I asked him that and he gave a funny kind of a laugh, and the other men joined in. It had begun to rain by this time and we'd all gone inside John O'Connell's, and it was he who answered me. He said it was a receptacle hidden in the side of a mountain where bad fellows brewed themselves poteen out of potatoes, instead of coming to his place and getting their spirits over the counter like decent Christians. Well, Black Michael and his friends drank a lot of this stuff together, and afterwards Black Michael wandered away with a keg of it that they'd given him, and he went on drinking until at last he fell asleep in a little dell at the top of the mountain. And when he woke up, he was listening to the

16

music of the Green-coated Boy. And all around there were the blue mountains, and the sun just rising over them, and a little clear stream running through the valley, and foxgloves growing beside it, and harebells, and great bunches of white and red heather, and the birds singing as if the dawn had made them mad, he said. And there was a little cabin built of rock down by the stream, and all round it, black goats of all sizes jumping about. It was the smell of them as much as the music that woke him up, Michael said, for he'd never known a place smell of anything so strong. But if they smelt awful, they were the loveliest goats you ever saw—even prettier than Amalthea, he said—in fact, you felt it was a place where you might meet a veritable Prince of Pucks."

Dominic stopped and looked at his twin, and from the rapt expression of her face decided that she had earned her reward. "And what do you think was the name of the place?"

"Ulphin!" she whispered.

"Yes, it was Ulphin," Dominic answered, "and it was about Ulphin that the boy was singing, for there were words to that tune, and Miley even sang a little bit of his song, only I can't remember how it went, or the words either. But there was something about

> *A land of beauty, a land of truth,*
> *Where youth shall never grow old, or pine.*

"But where is this land, Ulphin?" Josephine wanted to know. "How do we find it?"

"I asked Miley that, of course," Dominic answered, "but all he would say was 'Down the river and over the hill'."

"Down the river and over the hill!" Josephine echoed. "That must be our river, the Shannon. But I don't think he can have meant these hills. Slieve Anierin is a mountain, and besides it's right away, where the river begins."

"Wouldn't you like to have one of those lovely black goats?" Dominic asked her, and she thought how easy and likely he made it sound.

"Oh yes," Josephine cried, "and then he could marry

Amalthea and we'd have some wonderful baby kids." For she was a true woman in that she always thought of tomorrow where Dominic thought only of today.

Just then Nellie put her head round the door to remind the children that it was milking time. She had taught both of them to milk, but it was Josephine she called.

"But it's my turn with Amalthea today," Dominic said at once. "Don't you remember I fetched her back from Miss Morrissey's before tea?"

"Ah, but just see the rain!" Nellie answered. "Miss Josephine's school mack is a good one, but it's destroyed is yours with all the storms of the world, and yourself a good size too big for it and all. No, you cannot go in it to milk the goat this night."

Dominic stuck his jaw out but there was no gainsaying Nellie.

"He should have a new one then," said Josephine, giving Nellie a very straight look as she went out.

When she came in from milking, Nellie had started on the ironing, but Dominic had disappeared.

" 'Tis true," Nellie began a little apologetically, "the boy needs a better mackintosh. Sister Theresa at the convent was telling me there was a lot of very good clothing going with all the rest in the Major's sale up at the Demesne tomorrow. Maybe there might be a mack amongst them. The poor Major was only a small little man and Dominic indeed a well-grown child for his age." Josephine preened herself, knowing that she too had been paid a compliment. "I wonder now if your uncle was to give you ten shillings, would I trust you to buy one that was not rotten nor gone in the seams? 'Tis not I can go with you, for Jimmy Lyons has promised to take me with him to the town, and tomorrow my day off and all."

Josephine was a little daunted at the thought of attending a sale, an affair of which she had only the vaguest idea, alone with Dominic, but she knew that if Jimmy Lyons had any part in Nellie's plans for her day off, then the thing was

serious. It was Jim Lyons who took Miss Morrissey's milk to
the Creamery, and the two children liked riding with him
on the asses' cart with the burnished churns racketing along
behind. Dominic, who studied the classics with Uncle Theo,
said it was like a Roman chariot race as they swept round
the houses, and Josephine, who was learning the Old Testa-
ment at school, said it was like the hosts of the Egyptians
following after the children of Israel.

Jimmy Lyons was a celebrated cross-country runner. He
was a little fellow with a face like a frog, a small body and
long legs, and he lived with his mother and an invalid
brother. Mrs. Lyons, who was the village postmistress, walked
twelve miles every day to deliver the letters, and although
she was well over seventy, she was a noted step-dancer, had
a foot as light as a fairy, and never missed a dance at the
cross-roads. But Jim's only capital was the cups he had won
by his running, and the girls were a bit stand-offish with him,
excepting only Nellie. Jim, who was a Protestant, had several
times invited the Rector to arrange a match for him with her.
But whether the Rector had a poor memory for such matters,
or felt it was not for him to interfere in the workings of Pro-
vidence, or whether he bethought him that Nellie had a way
with her cooking and he might search in vain for her like,
the thing had not made much progress, and Dominic had
often told Jim, as one man to another, that in pressing his
suit with the Rector he was barking up the wrong tree.

Perhaps, thought Josephine, tomorrow Nellie would take
matters into her own hands and a solution would be found.
So she agreed that if Uncle Theo could be persuaded by
Nellie to hand out a ten-shilling note, she would go with
Dominic to the late Major's sale and bid for the best mackintosh that that sum could buy. Nellie, for her part, promised
to make them some sausage rolls for a picnic lunch, and
Josephine left her hurrying through her ironing so as to have
time to make them before supper, as she herself went out to
try to find the place where Torty the cat had hidden her
new kittens. She never discovered them but in the apple

chamber she did find Dominic who, looking for the kittens, had found the apples. She told him of all these very important plans and the doubtless very desirable mackintosh that awaited him at the end of them.

"If it's the one the Major wore to go fishing on the lough," observed Dominic, "I thought it looked a very shabby old one when we first came here, and I don't suppose it's looking any better now."

"Perhaps it won't be that one at all," said Josephine consolingly. "Perhaps it will be a nice new one that he kept for best, when he went to the races."

But Dominic only grunted.

CHAPTER II

The Sale at the Demesne

That summer it was always raining. The next day it was no better. Slieve Aneurin had disappeared behind a grey curtain of cloud and a fine rain was falling. Nellie sent word to Jim Lyons that she would not be going out with him but he could have tea with her in the Rectory kitchen instead. First of all, however, he was to drive the two children the four miles to the Demesne and, as she would not be needing it herself, Dominic could borrow her mackintosh, which would save him from getting too bad a wetting.

Dominic was furious. "I shan't go at all," he declared. "Fancy having to stand up and make my bid in a thing that buttons up on the wrong side and has a blue hood! Everyone there will know it's Nellie's mackintosh I'm wearing!"

"But surely, it would be still worse if they thought it was your own," argued Josephine in an effort to be consoling. "Besides, you've only got to wear it until you buy your new one."

"It's sure to be grand and cost far more than ten shillings," Dominic objected gloomily, "or else it will be some awful old thing even worse than Nellie's."

But when Nellie came in to tell them that Jimmy Lyons was waiting for them in the courtyard, the prospect of a ride in the asses' cart was so much more tempting than that of watching the rain falling past the kitchen windows that

Dominic allowed Nellie to help him on with the hated garment and led the way out to the courtyard with no further objections.

"Is it at the gate of the Demesne that I'm to leave you?" Jim asked, quite impressed by the importance of the occasion. "Faix, they do be telling me there's great goings on there today. For it's well known the poor Major was a well-travelled gentleman and it's all the lands of the East he's after travelling through till he'd come to the back of the sun, and all the folks there as black as your shadow. And wherever his way has led him, he'll have found something quare to bring home to put into his collection; maybe an old sword, the end of it still covered all over wid poison and blood, or maybe a brass tray, and all the gods of the heathen on it, or a great flat bell wid a booming voice 'twould make your heart sink to listen to. Och, there's wonders enough to make a fun fair up at the Major's, and it's no lie I'm telling ye, for I had it from my Aunt Sara, and she up there two nights past or three to lay the poor man out."

When they reached the gates of the Demesne, sure enough they found a great stir; cars coming in and cattle trucks too, for the Major had a famous herd of Kerry cows as well as some pigs, a draught horse or two and even a couple of old hunters that everybody was anxious to give a good home to. There were men in dogcarts, boys on bicycles, the local priest and quite a few farmers in their asses' carts, with whom Jimmy exchanged greetings. And a Garda was there, telling everybody which way they should come in, or park their cars, or where the horses and asses had best be tied up.

It was all very lively and gay, except, of course, for the rain which was busy plastering Josephine's hair to her head. But as Dominic started to walk up the long drive, beside which the river flowed, with Josephine, the thought of Nellie's mackintosh came back to him and all the great crowds that would see him in it, and you could see that there was bitterness in his heart.

"How boring everything is!" he burst out, kicking a stone

with fury out of his way. And Josephine, looking in his face, knew that she must be careful how she answered him, for to tell an angry man that life is wonderful when his mind is bent on wrath is to have the anger turned against yourself. Instead she gave him the kind of look that one twin some-

times gives the other when they have nothing in the world but each other and the goat. "It won't always be like this," she said. "Some day they'll come back, and when they find that we haven't ever touched any cows' milk, they'll take us

23

with them next time. And oh, look, Dominic, at that man standing up amongst all the pigs with a hammer in his hand! Whatever do you think he's going to do to them?"

There seemed, indeed, to be two quite different sales going on; one at the farm, the entrance by which the children had arrived, whence came noises of uneasy lowings and squealings, and the other in the house and a partly covered-in courtyard between the house and the farm. It was here that the bulk of the Major's collections appeared to be temporarily housed and into this courtyard, attracted by so many strange and interesting objects, the children quickly passed. But Josephine was not long in deciding that it was in the house itself that the Major's wardrobe was most likely to be on view. Sure enough, in a long corridor at the back of the house they came upon sundry tweed overcoats, ulsters and riding breeches, along with some fishing tackle and waders and amongst it all, and Dominic's eye was quick to pick it out, a little bundle of burberries and mackintoshes.

"I don't care for this one much," Dominic said, hauling out what proved to be a long waterproof cape marked with a ticket 'Lot 72'.

"Do you think this one is nicer?" asked Josephine, offering him a very stiff, hardly worn yellow oilskin.

"No, I'd never want to dress in yellow," Dominic replied coldly. "But that one beneath the dark overcoat—let's have a look at that."

Dominic had it by the scruff of the neck; the twins tugged together and out came a garment that was so eminently the kind of mackintosh he might have dreamed of that Dominic felt certain it would fetch a price far beyond the range of Uncle Theo's ten-shilling note . . . until they pulled the second sleeve clear, and then they saw a great smear of green paint all down it from shoulder to cuff, like a gigantic note of interrogation.

"Just look!" Dominic cried, feeling quite guilty on the Major's behalf. "However can he have done that?"

A lanky cold-looking man who was holding up a grey check

ulster in front of himself to see how much of him it covered,
hearing Dominic's exclamation, put the ulster back on its
pile and gave his attention to Lot 69, which was the number
of the painted mackintosh.

"How could he have done it!" he echoed. "Wasn't it the
Major could never leave his boats alone but would always be
giving them a silver line here and a dab of paint there, till
it's a clear wonder, by the Holy, he hasn't the whole of his
coat painted over and not the sleeve only! And a nice elegant
coat it is, sure, that any one would be proud to be seen about
in and the sleeve maybe hidden on the farther side. If I was
a smaller man, by damn, I'd bid for it myself, but it's not I
could look my best in any of the Major's togs, excepting
maybe this old coat." And he turned back to the grey ulster
and attempted to regard his own reflection in the window
over his shoulder.

Before Dominic had time to follow suit with Lot 69, there
was a stir at the far end of the passageway, and it was seen
that one of the auctioneers had now entered the room, followed by a miscellaneous crowd of men, women and boys,
each of whom seemed to be in a more or less successfully
concealed state of excitement. Dominic, meeting their casual
and preoccupied glances, was relieved to find that after all
no one seemed to look at Nellie's mack as if they had seen it
before and that, with few exceptions, the costumes the other
buyers had chosen to don this rainy day were quite as
eccentric as his own.

"Now ladies and gentlemen," the auctioneer was saying,
"we come to Lot 44, a steel engraving of a picture entitled
'The Thin Red Line' by Lady Butler. If you've a damp patch
on the wall it's just the very thing for it. What may I say for
this very stirring picture? Start me off, please! Ten shillings?
Five shillings then. A maiden bid from the lady on my left."
The children saw that Mrs. Markham, a very important lady
who with her two henpecked sons had lately come to live
near the Rectory because she considered Earlscourt a slum,
had put up her hand. Rap, and the auctioneer's hammer fell.

THE SALE AT THE DEMESNE

" 'The Thin Red Line' to this lady for five shillings. Now here we have an enamel pail and ditto jug and bowl. 'Twill keep the baby tidy. Did I hear eighteen pence bid over there?" Rap again. The junior vet, a bachelor, who had a place of his own and bred blood horses, was heard quickly explaining that he never had enough bowls and basins for bathing his damaged patients. Very soon the auctioneer was approaching the pile of garments beside which the twins were standing. They saw the gleam of triumph and the chill face light up as the grey ulster was knocked down to their old friend at twelve shillings and sixpence, and a moment later it was the turn of Lot 69.

"Now here, gentlemen, is a stout mackintosh; the very thing for the summer holidays. Now this is really a very high-class garment. We all know there was never a smarter man than the Major when he was going to the Horse Show or the Punchestown Races. Well I mind seeing him in this very mack coming home with a smile on his face and all the notes crackling in his pocket. What may I say for this? Start me off at a pound, somebody!"

"It's got a great smear of paint all over one sleeve!" choked Dominic, seeing his mackintosh disappear before ever he had owned it. The auctioneer shot him a vicious glance.

" 'Tis true," he said, "as this young gentleman has kindly pointed out, there is a little daub of paint on the left-hand sleeve—the left-hand one, mark you, so that you can shake your man by the hand and turn you round, and no one a penny the wiser. Or take it to the wife tonight; show her what a good coat you're after buying at the sale and ask her for a little drop of turps. She'll think you're the smartest chap that ever went to a sale. One pound, may I say? Well, fifteen shillings then."

"Ten shillings," Dominic uttered in a voice that trembled. There was a silence that seemed to shake the heavens.

"No more than ten shillings for this very high-class mack?"

The auctioneer looked round. His heart seemed pierced, and Josephine felt quite sorry for him.

THE SALE AT THE DEMESNE

The hammer fell and the auctioneer brightened. "If you wish to pay in cash for it," he addressed Dominic, "you can settle at once with my clerk here, and you can take it away without waiting for the end so."

This suited Dominic very well, for now he could hardly wait to be parted from the blue hood. Uncle Theo's note was handed over and Dominic entered into possession.

Their friend, now looking quite cosy in his ulster, came round to offer congratulations.

"Slip it on, boy," he urged, "let me see if it will fit ye." And he helped Dominic on with the painted mackintosh.

Perhaps it hung a little loosely on Dominic's rather skinny figure, the sleeves a hint too long, but as the man remarked and the twins agreed, "'twould allow all the more elbow room for growth." And as for buying some turps for the sleeve, "Do you know," Dominic told them, "I think I'll keep the old mack as it is. With the green paint on it I'd pick it out from a hundred others at school and always know it for my own."

Smiling, he thrust his hands deeply into the pockets. "Why, here's an old bit of paper." He brought his right hand out and in it a one-pound note.

There was an awed silence.

"Dang me if it isn't just as the man said," cried their friend in the ulster. "The Major coming smiling home from the races and in his pockets a handful of notes. Is it not the lucky boy ye are this day!"

"But it isn't Dominic's. Oughtn't he to give it back?" asked Josephine, fidgeting a little, for they had been brought up to have a healthy respect for the law.

"Give it back? And who to!" their friend mocked. "The Major's gone where money's nothing but an encumbrance. If ye could get it to him, it's no kindness at all ye'd be doing him in the eyes of the Saints. It's they would turn their eyes up, one and all, and be talking of th'auld camel and the needle's eye, and the poor Major shamed before them all!"

The children took his point. "But his family," Josephine objected, "oughtn't we to give it back to them?"

27

THE SALE AT THE DEMESNE

"By the Powers, the Major had no family. He was never one for the women, I'm telling you. He'd meet them willingly when he was asked down to the Canon's for a cup of tea, but ne'er a one would he ask to his house. Och, he was a wily one, was the Major!" And the Major's ulster seemed to heave and shake with amusement.

Josephine was silenced and Dominic eyed her with displeasure. "Meddlesome Matty!" was all he said. "Now let's go back to the courtyard and have a look at all that collection the Major brought back from his travels. I shouldn't wonder if I didn't start a collection too." And Dominic fingered the Major's note lovingly.

So Josephine swallowed her conscientious scruples and followed where Dominic led the way into the courtyard, where the noise of the hammer and its accompanying chorus retreated into the fastnesses of the house.

What fascinating things the Major's collections contained! There were rook rifles, sets of chessmen, harness, camel bells, white elephants beautifully modelled in porcelain—Dominic and Josephine wanted to buy them all.

At first their attention was caught by a pair of assagai hanging crosswise in the outer hall.

"Those must be the spears Jim Lyons was telling us about," Dominic mused, running his thumb across their points.

"But don't you remember he said they were poisoned!" cried Josephine, snatching his hand away.

This would have started a wrangle had not Dominic at that moment spied an inkstand made from a horse's hoof, which immediately caught his fancy. "I shall bid for this," he said.

"But look at all those books it's standing on," Josephine pointed out. "It looks as if you've got to buy them too."

It seemed, indeed, as if Lot 264 included the whole set of the Waverley Novels, handsomely bound in morocco. "I shall just leave them behind," Dominic replied decisively and passed on to a pair of antique brass pistols curiously chased. The next moment he was acting showman to a long-armed Polynesian marionette whose joints worked by means of two slender sticks attached to its hands. "Here's the Queen of the Cannibal Islands," he cried, whilst the marionette in the accents of the sergeant at Dominic's school, cried out: "Arms bend, stretch, one, two, three, four!"

Then, just beyond the gesticulating marionette, their eyes glimpsed something together; a long elaborately carved canoe in which sat half a score of savages, each one armed with a spear and shield. It was complete though parts of it were broken and some of the elaborate trappings had come unstuck.

"Oh Dominic," Josephine cried, "did you ever see such a pretty ship. Look at their top-knots and feathers and the tufts on their shields. We'd never get that for ten shillings, would we?"

"I don't know," Dominic answered, breathing hard. "It's broken, but nothing that I couldn't mend myself with a little glue. You can tell it's a war canoe by all those shields and spears the crew are carrying."

At this moment there was a shuffling of footsteps and the voice of the auctioneer was once more heard in their close proximity. He was now dealing with a good many dusty old bottles of wine which were apparently the material of another of the Major's collections.

Dominic and Josephine, who were little interested in the Major's choice of wine or its ultimate ownership, were at last recalled to the present by some very excitable bidding between Mrs. Markham and the vet's mother for a croquet set in a heavy wooden case. This eventually fell to Mrs. Markham and the children heard her tell the auctioneer's clerk that one of the young gentlemen would call for it on Monday. The groan given by these two lanky youths was distinctly audible from where the children stood.

Suddenly Dominic shot bolt upright, his eyes fixed on the auctioneer's rostrum. "This very ingenious canoe . . ." the auctioneer's voice had come floating towards them. "We all know . . . the Major . . . a great traveller. Gentlemen, which of you is for adventure? May I say ten shillings?"

"Yes, you may," came Dominic's answer, his voice sharply penetrating the distance between them.

The auctioneer smiled across at him. "Ten shillings I'm bid. Any advance on ten shillings for this very fine canoe, in perfect condition, so I'm assured. Any of you can examine it. Any advance on ten shillings?"

Not a voice rose. Not so much as a head was nodded. "Come on, gentlemen, any advance at all?" the auctioneer repeated impatiently and a moment later the hammer had fallen. "The canoe goes to this young gentleman," he said and then, leaning in Dominic's direction, "Will you come and fetch it any time after three o'clock when the sale ends?" he added, and passed on to the next thing.

"Now here's a very pretty French clock; one of the choicest pieces in the Major's collection," he began. "It is said to keep excellent time once a pair of hands has been added." But already the children had turned back to the war canoe, feeling that they could now give full rein to their admiration of their possession.

"I wish he'd let us pay for it and take it away with us," said Dominic regretfully.

"What's the time now?" Josephine asked.

"As the clock hadn't any hands, I don't know," Dominic answered. The children looked at each other and then at the bulging packages that Nellie had packed in their school satchels. In their hearts they felt very well satisfied with life and with their two purchases. Suddenly sausage rolls became more important than anything else in the Major's collection.

"If we go and eat our lunch now," said Josephine, "it will make three o'clock come all the quicker. And look, the rain has stopped at last and there's the sun coming out!"

The twins left the Demesne by the way they had entered it, on their way meeting Canon Pennyfeather driving his car very fast because, although he knew that the Major's sale was on a Saturday, he had been under the impression, until his laundry unexpectedly returned, that today was only Thursday. But as he was too absent-minded to have noticed that all his tires were flat, his progress was erratic and he missed Josephine by inches.

Soon they were seated on the sunny side of the old stone bridge that crossed the Shannon in the center of the village, munching their sausage rolls and the sticky jam sandwiches with which Nellie had accompanied them. "I'll tell you what," said Dominic happily, "after we've fetched the canoe away, let's bring it here and float it on the stream."

"Oh yes, so long as the current doesn't carry it away," Josephine added.

"Then we'll make a dam across the shallow part and build it a little harbor," said Dominic.

No sooner said than done. Shoes and stockings were whipped off and in this intoxicating pastime time itself was forgotten. No fish that played in the stream, not even Canon Pennyfeather himself, could have regarded it less.

CHAPTER III

An Anti-Climax

The afternoon deepened. The rays of light that fell through the trees upon the river had begun to slant. Already several cars laden with household effects had crossed the bridge. Beneath it the children wading in the river stood up, looked at the sun and began to wonder whether in the Major's garden it was yet three o'clock. Hurriedly pulling stockings over wet feet, they hastened back to the white gates to claim their war canoe and bring it back to the harbor that was ready for it at last.

They crossed to the farm where sundry cattle and pigs, each marked with a white ticket, were being hustled into cattle trucks, and entered the courtyard where only a scattering of the Major's treasures now remained. Filled with apprehension, they sought their canoe in the place where they had last seen it. The trestle table on which it had stood was empty save for the marionette which lay, looking rather like a dead bird, a tumbled heap out of which the long eyes set in the chalk-white face seemed to watch them enigmatically.

"That clerk has probably moved it somewhere else to be ready for us," said Josephine and they hurried across to where two men were carrying the auctioneer's rostrum towards the entrance drive. In one of them the children recognized the auctioneer's clerk.

"Where's our canoe?" Dominic demanded, falling into step beside the man's rather crab-like progress.

AN ANTI-CLIMAX

"What's that ye're saying, me boy?" There was a moment's pause as over his shoulders the auctioneer's clerk, a heavily built man with a sparse reddish stubble, looked vaguely at the two children.

"Our canoe. We bought it, don't you remember? for ten shillings?"

"Och, the folding canoe, is it? 'Tis there yonder against the farther wall." The auctioneer's clerk made a backward motion of the head towards where, under a chestnut tree that grew on the far side of the courtyard, a large assortment of miscellaneous objects were gathered together into a pile waiting for their owners to claim them.

"A folding canoe, did he say?" Josephine was asking a few moments later as they began their search amongst these objects. "What did he mean by that?"

"I can't imagine," answered Dominic who was beginning to look very anxious. "I wish we'd come back sooner. I shouldn't wonder if somebody else hasn't grabbed it on the quiet, when the auctioneer's clerk wasn't looking."

At this point the man in question, having deposited the rostrum in a waiting van, was seen approaching at a leisurely pace.

"Oh please," the two children hailed him simultaneously, "where did you say our canoe was? We can't find it anywhere!"

"Indeed then, it's because you've no eyes to your heads. A canoe, is it? And what do you call this?" The auctioneer's clerk led them back to the pile and pointed to a something that in their eyes somewhat resembled a curragh they had once seen lying on the shore in County Clare, that is to say that it had a skin made of some supple material lightly stretched across a backbone and ribs made of flexible spars. Though its deck was partly covered in, beneath it lay a thick layer of dust, dead leaves, cobwebs and all the alien matter that accumulates through the years upon a hollow object that has lain long in an open shed.

"That's not our canoe," said Dominic looking at it in

33

AN ANTI-CLIMAX

angry disgust, feeling that some ghastly and probably irremediable mistake had been perpetrated at their expense.

The auctioneer's clerk pulled a dog-eared catalogue out of his breast pocket. "Lot 426," he read out, "a Klepper canoe with two double paddles, knocked down to the Rectory children—that's yourselves, is it not? for ten shillings."

"That's us," Dominic agreed, "but it's not the canoe we bought. It was a little model; a sort of war canoe, over there, on that trestle table." He pointed to where, looking more like a shot partridge than ever, the marionette's white face peeked out from its tumbled brown heap of dress and limb.

"But this was the one ye bid for!" The auctioneer's clerk's face wore a horribly assured look, but in it a light seemed suddenly to shine. "I mind now the one ye're meaning," he cried, and as suddenly his face fell. "But that was another lot, towards the end of the sale." He licked his thumb and shuffled over the leaves of the catalogue.

"Arrah now, here 'tis. Lot 708. Miscellaneous curios, and there was a dozen or so of them if I'm not mistaken, and we only selling them one half-hour or so ago. 'Twas before dinner-time this canoe was sold, and you it was who made the winning bid; I remember it well. And the little toy boat," he continued, "went just now to an auld gentleman who bought it and all the rest of them for his grandson. He wouldn't take th'auld doll; said his grandson wouldn't thank him for it and he'd leave it behind so. Ye can take it and welcome if that was the Lot ye fancied."

Dominic looked at him with sick scorn but vouchsafed no other reply. "To think," he burst out to Josephine, "we've been spending our afternoon making that harbor and all the time our canoe was being sold under our noses! It's—it's —it's an anti-climax, that's what it is!"

It was a word he had brought into his last English essay before the holidays—an essay that had earned him top marks, and he used it now with a feeling of great satisfaction; a new tool to carve out his exact sense. He looked at Josephine, seeking to meet in her eyes a despair equal to his own.

But she was bending down over the old hull, her eyes invisible upon it. She passed a finger along the skin that covered it. She looked at the two long double paddles that lay inside. In a flash she saw those paddles, one in her own hands, the other in Dominic's. Here, she believed, was something that they could do together.

"It seems to me," she said very slowly, "that if it's an anti-climax, whatever that is, it's a rather exciting one."

Dominic's feelings seemed to pull themselves up short. He approached the drab old hulk and stood beside Josephine, peering into its depths. He saw the two paddles, the handles worn smooth in many voyages, and then, lying amongst the shadows, something else. Plunging a hand into the cobwebs he drew out what seemed to be a fair-sized and rather weighty canvas bag. Under the eyes of the auctioneer's clerk, now popping out of his head with curiosity, he and Josephine laid it on the grass and untied the dirty tapes that bound it. There emerged, rolled in a ground-sheet, a bulky something, pale green in color and with two pointed sticks, a number of what looked like meat skewers, and a few odd ropes.

"It's a tent!" cried Dominic, now thoroughly intrigued.

"Eh now, there might have been another ten shillings for the Major," interposed the auctioneer's clerk, and for a moment the children feared he was about to claim it.

"The Major's much better without it where he's gone," Josephine hastened to tell him, her mind on all those disapproving angels, and turned back to the canvas bag. "And look, Dominic, there's something hard—two things, no three!" She pulled out a tiny kettle, a cork in its mouth, a minute spirit-lamp and a grimy jam-pot and inside it a very ancient box of safety matches.

"So that they'd never get wet," Dominic cried. "What a good idea!"

"Arrah, the Major, he seems to have been one with a mind to everything!" The auctioneer's clerk was becoming quite envious. "And it's you is the lucky ones today, wid your boat and your house and now your cooking-pots an' all. And you that was breaking your hearts over the loss of a little toy! You'll be going to sea now surely, Captain and Mate, may God preserve you, making the journey down the Shannon maybe, and thinking nothing of it, a great boy and girl like yourselves!"

Dominic turned a long and thoughtful gaze on the auctioneer's clerk. "I shouldn't be surprised," he said coolly. "But first of all, what I want to know is, where we can leave it for tonight?"

"And why wouldn't you leave it where it is?" the man demanded. "There's a croquet set that was knocked down to Mrs. Markham that the two poor young gentlemen will be carrying home between them on Monday, God aid them! There's none would have a mind to steal such things, and the sabbath coming in between. If it wasn't the wrong way of the stream, you could have paddled the old boat the most of the way to your own place, but maybe there's a farmer with an asses' cart somewhere would carry it out for ye. God in Heaven, is that not the lorry I'm keeping waiting!" A loud honking noise had been heard from the drive. "Will I collect the ten shillings from ye now, for that's the last I have owing."

Dominic received a ten-shilling note in exchange for the late Major's pound, and the two children prepared to make their way home. Only Josephine as she turned to go caught what she felt to be a very pathetic look from a white face that looked out from a heap of rags. Now that the marionette had been offered to them, it seemed like a betrayal to leave it there. She snatched it up, looking a little self-conscious as she met Dominic's gaze, but Dominic was too happy to give more than a rather cynical smile.

"She'll remind us of the war canoe that was nearly ours," he allowed.

"Do you still wish we'd got it instead of this?" his sister asked.

Dominic swallowed. "I wish we'd got them both," he said.

36

"But the other ten shillings?" Josephine reminded him. "It might be very useful."

"I'm quite sure it will," Dominic answered, and his eyes took on a preoccupied yet ardent look that Josephine knew well; that had sometimes proved a prelude to some new adventure.

"What are you thinking about, Dominic?" she asked him.

But Dominic was in one of his provoking moods. "Perhaps I'll tell you," he said and paused; "the day after tomorrow."

Josephine's face fell.

"I'll tell you what," he said, and now he was smiling. "If you'll come back here with me tomorrow, and help me to clean the old boat up, I'll tell you tomorrow. There!"

So of course Josephine agreed to come and as they walked home together they decided that it would be better not to say anything at all about today's doings. Not even to Nellie, they agreed.

"We'll just tell her," said Josephine, "how we bought the painted mackintosh. And after all, that was the beginning of it all."

CHAPTER IV

The Canoe

That was the beginning of it all. But when they got back, Nellie seemed too much taken up with the events of the day, whatever they may have been, to have much interest to spare for any affairs but her own. She did not even notice that striking smear of paint on Dominic's new mackintosh till he showed it to her himself and even then she could not rid herself of the conviction that Dominic himself was somehow responsible for it, "messing about amongst the Major's paint pots, the stupid careless boy!"

"But it was the Major painting his boats who was the stupid careless boy," Dominic pointed out, "and you know, Nellie, there's a Latin proverb that says you mustn't speak ill of the dead."

"And will you spare us hearkening to such blasphemious talk!" said Nellie who felt that the only proper placc for Latin proverbs was the inside of a church. Nor would she so much as smile when Josephine showed her the marionette and even gave a demonstration of the working of those eloquent hands.

"An auld doll!" she said gazing at it woodenly. "Do ye think it was for that that I plagued your uncle for the sake of that ten-shilling note?"

"She was *given* to us," Josephine replied with dignity.

38

And look, Nellie, she's going on her knees before you now to ask you for John the Baptist's head."

"Devil take the child!" cried Nellie, springing away from the marionette as though it were a cockatrice. "Will ye be ceasing from such ungodly talk. And let you not be leaving that heathenish thing in my kitchen or I might be in need of a fire-lighter one day and she already there beside me!"

Josephine took the hint and hurried her marionette upstairs to make it a home in the bottom of her chest of drawers, a region to which Nellie seldom penetrated. On her return to the kitchen she found Nellie telling Dominic that, the next afternoon being Sunday, she was going with Jim Lyons to drink a friendly cup of tea with his mother, and the children exchanged glances for they knew that, with Nellie out of the way, the afternoon would be their own. But Nellie, looking rather bothered, was to lighten their hearts still further. "If Jim's mother is agreeable," she told them, "though I can see 'tis an uneasy mind he has for putting such questions to th'auld woman, we thought of waiting no longer but of going to see the lawyer the very next day. Your uncle would surely spare me the day off Monday, Saturday being so wet and all, and who knows there might be a bit of wedding cake for all of us before the year is out!"

"Oh Nellie," cried Dominic, looking quite put out, "are you sure you aren't being rather hasty?"

Josephine could hardly believe her ears at hearing her twin talk in this fashion after all the many times he had railed against Jimmy Lyons for the slowness of his pace in courting. And she told Nellie that she for her part felt that seven years was ample time for Jim to make up his mind. "And besides, I love wedding cake," she added.

"So do I!" said Dominic. And she wondered the more.

For the rest of the evening Nellie busied herself washing and ironing her white satin blouse with the pearl buttons, and stitching a large blue bow on to her hat, so that Josephine felt that that cup of tea, however friendly, was also to be a rather critical one.

THE CANOE

When Sunday afternoon came, the children were very glad
Nellie was not there to see where the kitchen bucket, a cake
of soap and Nellie's best scrubbing-brush were off to in Dominic's hand as they legged it along the road to the Demesne.

Once the rubbish was emptied out of her, it was wonderful
to see how quickly their boat assumed a different personality.
Her lines were always graceful but now it became apparent
that under the overlying dust a silvery skin had been concealed; a skin in which no amount of scubbing revealed the
smallest blemish. There were two little seats to be attached
to bars that fitted into slots. Forward and aft, under cover of
the half-deck, immense cavities were revealed where the
Major must have kept his stores, for there was still an un-
opened tin labelled Osborn Biscuits in the farthest point of
the bows. It was these cavities that Nellie's scrubbing-brush
now explored, and it was fortunate for the children that the
river Shannon flowed so close to the spot where the canoe
lay, for at one time it seemed as though all Shannon's waters
would never be enough to complete that heroic wash. But
they scrubbed and they rinsed and the sun came out and
added his bright polish to their work and at last as they sat
back on their heels and contemplated the result they found
it difficult to believe that she was really theirs, the Major's
old canoe their own dazzling possession.

"Let's get inside it," Josephine suggested, "and see how it
feels to put to sea."

Gingerly stepping on the ribs so as not to harm the silver
skin, they stepped aboard. Dominic seized one of the paddles
jettisoned during the clean-up, handed the other to Josephine
and they dipped them into the waving grasses of the meadow.

"But we must learn to pull together," Dominic adjured his
twin. "Look now, I'm in the bows and we're facing the way
we're going. Watch me, and when I dip my right paddle,
you dip yours and then the left, keeping time with me." They
swung the double paddles together and presently had estab-
lished some sort of unsteady floundering rhythm.

Dominic's laugh rang out like a song of triumph. "That'll

40

do for now," he said. "Shall I tell you where I'm going tomorrow?"

"You're going to Ulphin," she answered immediately.

For once he was taken aback. "How . . ." he began.

"I've guessed," she answered quickly, "and I'm coming with you."

Girls were too quick, thought Dominic. By some unfair act of divination they left you behind.

"Don't leave me behind!" she pleaded. There she was again! He turned and gave her a searching look. Her eyes were candid; as full of questions as his own. He thought of telling her that it would be too far, that she would get tired, that she would delay him.

"Two of us paddling would get along quicker than one," she said. "I won't be a nuisance. Really, Dominic."

Perhaps there was something in what she said. He saw them flying together through the water, their wet paddles glistening as the drops rolled back into the river. He saw the camp fire at night—she was better at fires than he was—not lonely any more, or rather frightening as he had imagined it.

"There's just one thing," she said. "Are you quite sure there really is an Ulphin?"

"Didn't I tell you Miley said there was?" he answered fiercely.

"Nobody might tell us how to find it."

"But Miley did tell me. Down the river and over the hill, he said. We've only got to go on down the river until we come to it."

"And how shall we know from the river what's over the hill?" she asked, uncertain still.

"Because of the *smell*," he uttered very impressively, and sniffed as though that scent were already on the wind. "We'd only have to follow our noses until we got to it."

"And when we get there," she insisted, "how are we going to bring our billy-goat home again? He would never stay in the canoe."

No, he hadn't thought of that. There was a pause. "I'm tired of all these boring questions," he said with impatience. "Who was it said they wanted to come?"

"Me," Josephine said. And she laughed. He decided to take her.

Though it was Sunday, Dominic had brought his ten-shilling note, knowing that once John O'Connell's was open, they would be denied nothing there or indeed in any other store that they might fancy for their journey. As they travelled the homeward road, Nellie's scrubbing-brush rattling in the empty bucket, they repeated over to each other, alphabetically arranged so as not to forget them, the various stores they would buy.

"Bacon," began Dominic.

"Bread, butter. What about baked beans?" Josephine took him up.

"Cheese, cornflakes, oh, and chocolate—what am I thinking of!" said Dominic.

They added potted meat, sardines and tea and then, as an afterthought, candles. "You never know with camping," Josephine said. "There might be burglars. When are we going to come home?" she asked her twin.

"In time for Nellie's wedding," he answered at once.

"But that might be quite a long time," she objected.

"I think the thing about cruises," said Dominic, "is that you never know."

They had to get in very quickly and very quietly. At any moment Uncle Theo might be coming in from evening service. He would not approve of their going shopping on Sunday and he would ask a great many questions about the things they had been buying—questions it might be quite difficult to answer. They entered the house by the kitchen which was empty, Nellie not yet returned from her tea-party, and they were making their way to the front of the house with the idea of unpacking the parcels in the bucket in Dominic's bedroom, when they heard their uncle's step in the kitchen, he having evidently followed them into the house.

"Dominic, Josephine!" they heard his voice calling as he approached.

They hesitated, in the act of pulling aside the heavy curtain which divided the servants' quarters from the rest of the house. Beside them was a door leading down a steep flight of steps into the cellar.

Quick as thought, Dominic pulled Josephine inside this door and silently closed it. They heard their uncle's steps pass within a yard of where they stood and fade away into the front of the house.

When they had passed: "Why shouldn't we leave it here?" Dominic whispered. "It's a place where nobody ever comes except Uncle Theo when the Canon is coming to lunch."

"Do you mean here, just on top of the stairs?" Josephine asked. "Supposing he did come down to count his wine or something? He'd be sure to put his foot in the bucket and get mixed up with our stores."

"Well, we could put it at the foot of the steps," Dominic considered, "somewhere out of sight."

Josephine looked down into the darkness and shrank back. "Who's going to put it there?" she asked.

"Well . . . I can," he answered in a voice that he tried to make assured. And with one hand on the wall and the bucket in the other he started the downward journey. After a moment of hesitation Josephine decided to follow. At the sound of her movement behind him, Dominic started violently and dropped the bucket. At the sound of the bucket and its contents clattering to the floor, Josephine shrieked and all but fell off the steps. Dominic turned upon her a face that even in the darkness looked blanched. "You silly!" he hissed. "Now of course, he'll come back! Come on down as quickly as you can and we'll hide."

They had crept into the shelter of a large empty barrel when they heard the door open above and a shaft of light shone down. "Who's there?" Uncle Theo's voice demanded, a little quaveringly.

He must be listening to the throbbing of their hearts in the silence, Josephine thought. A spider seemed to run down her neck and she gave a shudder. Hardly moving, Dominic pinched her arm.

A mutter of words came from above. They had never heard their uncle swear but Dominic felt certain he was doing so now. Another moment's silence and then the door was quietly closed and they heard the key turn in the lock. The footsteps went on to the kitchen door, returned, passed and died away.

"Now what are we going to do?" said Dominic and he began to laugh. But Josephine narrowly missed bursting into tears.

"Stay here until we starve to death, I suppose," she said rather tremulously.

"Not with all those sardines and cornflakes," her twin reminded her. "And I think people in real want have even been known to eat candles," he added.

"Do you think if we both shouted together, he'd hear us?" Josephine asked.

"Yes, I'm sure he would. But before we do that, let's pick up all our parcels and put them back in the bucket," her twin suggested. "Then perhaps we shall think of something."

By now their eyes had grown accustomed to the darkness, which was faintly illuminated by a distant grating. They had nearly finished recovering their parcels when Josephine gave a muffled cry. "Oh Dominic, look over there!" and she clutched her brother's arm. "Do you see those two white feet walking across the floor!"

They huddled together whilst the white feet lightly, playfully danced across the cellar.

"Why, it's Torty," cried Dominic, "Torty's white legs! I wonder whatever she does down here?"

Torty greeted them with immense affection and they remembered that they had not seen her since the day before yesterday.

"Oh look!" cried Josephine again, pointing to a heap of sacking in a corner. And then they knew what Torty did down there. She had kittens. She had her own private entrance too, by a partly broken grating. As they watched her, she made her exit by it.

"Clever Torty!" Dominic cried. "I wonder if . . ." And he stumbled across the floor after her. Yes, the grating was loose as well as broken. A little working at it and he had pushed it upwards and away. Josephine followed. There was even room for the bucket.

That night as they sat at supper: "Do you know," said Uncle Theo, "I heard the strangest noises coming from the cellar this evening. I almost thought the house was haunted. I think it must be infested by rats."

"Oh, we know who infests it," the children answered, looking their brightest. "It's Torty. She's just been having kittens there."

"Oh, kittens," said their uncle a little dubiously. "Well, they must have very powerful lungs for such small animals."

"We watched her going out," said Josephine.

"We watched her coming out," Dominic corrected her.

Uncle Theo looked from one to the other, a very curious expression on his face. He seemed to attach great importance to the difference between coming and going. Afterwards they heard him go to the cellar door and try it. He came back looking even more mystified.

"I believe he *meant* to lock us in," said Dominic darkly afterwards. "I'm glad we're going to leave him tomorrow."

CHAPTER V

The Start

How co-operative the children were next morning! Nellie couldn't understand it at all. It would make it easier for her, they said, if they took a picnic lunch out. There were still some of Saturday's sausage rolls left over, and they themselves would help her to cut the sandwiches. Plenty of jam sandwiches, they said, and plenty of jam, as there was on Saturday and, yes, it would be lovely to have half the treacle tart she had made for the Rector's lunch. Sure, the dear man would never mind. He had been so very sympathetic about letting her change her day off. She wondered whether he would have acted as kindly had he known to what end that train of circumstances was to lead?

The smiling children waved Nellie off from the back door. "Now Nellie," Dominic had said, "take care you don't do anything rash!" But Josephine had run after her and flung her arms round her neck. "Dear Nellie," she had said as she hugged her. "I am sure you and Jimmy will be very happy." A queer little girl she was, sure. Nellie had quite a lump in her throat at the warmth of her farewell. Then, as she heard the wheels of Jim's asses' cart approaching the end of the Rectory drive, Nellie forgot all about the dear children and began to prepare herself for the two important interviews that lay before her. She rather thought she had won Jim's mother's compliance the day before. The old lady had admired the blue bow and said that it made Nellie look a little younger, but you could never tell with a woman like that one—a woman that wouldn't grow old.

The only one they let into the secret was the goat Amalthea. They were a long time saying good-bye to her and telling her of the wonderful company they would be keeping when they returned.

"There was one of them," Dominic told her, "Miley said he was a very Prince of Pucks—that seems to mean a billygoat. So if you married him, you'd count as a princess!"

"And your children would be of the Blood Royal," Josephine reminded her. "But I thought," she turned to Dominic, "I thought Puck was a fairy?"

"He might be a fairy," Dominic agreed, remembering his uncle's lessons and a certain faun about which he had had to learn a Latin poem, "and still be a sort of billy-goat."

"You believe in Ulphin, don't you, Amalthea?" Josephine asked her anxiously. And Amalthea nodded her head several times very quickly as is the way with goats.

"We'll each take a blanket off our beds to roll ourselves up in at night," Dominic said.

"And don't you think we could take that old carriage-rug from the chest at the end of the hall?" Josephine suggested. "Uncle Theo always lets us take it for picnics. And this counts as a picnic, doesn't it?"

"Oh, I'm quite sure it does," Dominic answered.

There was nobody about as they set out to walk to the Demesne; no one to ask them what was in that big bundle of bedding and stores slung over Dominic's shoulder, or the little bundle in which Josephine carried the lunch and a spare shirt and pair of shorts for each of them, two mackintoshes, one with a painted sleeve, and the marionette.

"We couldn't leave her behind," she protested in answer to Dominic's objections. "Not now we know Nellie's going to burn her for a heretic. It would be almost like conniving at a murder!"

They had no difficulty in carrying the canoe the short distance to the river. Here Dominic had an inspiration.

"Why shouldn't we use the marionette for our figure-head?" he suggested. "Ships often have figure-heads. She might be a sort of mascot and bring us luck!" He took a piece of string out of his pocket and had begun to tie the marionette's body to the bows before Josephine could think of any reason why he shouldn't. "You see, we'll leave her arms free," Dominic argued, "so that she'll be able to wave to all the passing traffic. There now, doesn't she look smashing!"

"We might have a collision and she might be smashed," said Josephine, too down-hearted about her charge to intend a joke.

This done, Dominic boarded the boat whilst Josephine handed down the two bundles they had brought with them and added the grimy bundle they had acquired with the canoe. This he settled in the bottom of the boat forward, as a seat for himself; he contrived a similar seat for Josephine out of the rugs and clothes, whilst the provisions were stowed away in the bows and stern.

Nobody saw them go. Only one lean solitary figure was in sight, and that one so bowed beneath the weight of a croquet set in a large wooden case that his eyes, they decided, were never once lifted in their direction. On the northern horizon Slieve Anierin, his head in a rainbow, looked down over the green plain and the slender river that divided it. Golden the fields were with ragwort and the row of hills in the near distance partaking of, but never quite matching, the river's deep blue. Far away were their uncle with his Irish texts; Nellie with her tyrannical ways. They tasted freedom, and it was a moment for ecstasy. In a silence unbroken save for the croak and drip of Dominic's paddle, they slid between the banks.

Soon Dominic rested on his paddle. "I thought as much,"

he said then, for the river was bearing them gently along. Swelled by the summer's rains, the little stream had a fast flow of water and all he had to do was to dip an occasional paddle to keep the canoe's bows straight. Encouraged by this Josephine decided that it was her turn to paddle, and found it immediately easier than she had imagined possible, and so, between drifting and paddling, they had soon put some distance between themselves and the Demesne.

"I wonder who will miss us first," Josephine meditated, idly watching the end of Dominic's paddle.

"Nellie, when she comes home tonight," Dominic guessed. "And at about the same time Uncle Theo will decide that we've gone to earth in the cellar again and perhaps go and unlock the door."

"I shouldn't think he'll bother," said Josephine. "But they won't know where else to look. Nellie'll be worried," she added.

"Not whilst her head is full of Jim's mother and the lawyer," Dominic answered.

"No, I think she'll still be worried," Josephine insisted.

The sun stood high overhead. Their throats were parched, their hands beginning to give warning of future blisters. It was extraordinarily quiet, the country stretching away from the river's brim unbroken by any sign of human habitation. There had been no passing traffic for the marionette to wave to; not so much as a fisherman on the bank.

Close to the river two goats were tethered. At sight of them the children's thirst increased. They still had three shillings and ninepence over from Dominic's ten-shilling note.

"There's a house in those bushes," said he. "Let's see if they'll sell us some milk."

They tied the canoe and walked across the bit of rushy grass to the cottage door. Of course they could have a glass of milk, said the woman who opened it. She had some by her now, but she would take no money for it.

"You're poor children and strangers, and I'm glad to give

it," she said. "See, I'll pour it into this lemonade bottle. No, don't take it from the girl!" she added to the child into whose hand Josephine had attempted to slip a sixpenny bit.

They cut hunks off the loaf of bread they had brought from home and ate it with the Galtee cheese from their store, and draughts of goat's milk completed the meal. Soon they were once more on their way.

The day growing hotter and their arms weary, they drifted with the current on into the afternoon, a little drowsy from the bright light reflected from the water and the river's minty sedgey smell. They were growing hungry again and thinking perhaps a little wistfully that at home it must be past tea-time when they came to a great ancient house, its walls rising out of the water.

They passed the house and then, just below it, came upon a place where the bank stood high and lightly wooded. Dominic leaned on his paddle and surveyed the shore. Josephine, following his glance, caught his eye and nodded.

"A camp for tonight?" said he.

"Yes, and a place for tea now," she answered.

They chose a hollow hidden from the house by the hill and the trees. Here Josephine built her fire whilst Dominic spread the ground-sheet and set up the Major's tent. When this was done and the kettle hung over the crackling flames, the landscape seemed entirely transformed.

"Do you know, Dominic," said Josephine contentedly, spreading butter on to bread, "we've made it into quite a little home by the river."

Dominic stopped hammering. "I wonder how many homes we shall make by the river before we get to Ulphin," he speculated.

Josephine sighed. The Shannon, she knew, was long and this home to her such a very sweet one, if rather small. "What shall we have for our tea?" she asked him then. "Potted meat, baked beans or sardines?"

He gazed at her across the fire. "Wouldn't scrambled eggs be lovely?" he suddenly asked.

How tiresome he was. "But we haven't any . . ." she was beginning to say when he jumped up.

"I believe this is some sort of a farm," he said. "Those cows we passed must belong here, because there aren't any other houses. I'll go and ask them if they've got any eggs for sale."

"The kettle isn't going to boil for ever so long," she said. "I'll come too."

Dominic led the way, clinking three shillings and ninepence importantly in his pocket. The path ran right round the back of the great house and past many outbuildings which seemed even more dilapidated than the house itself, the decayed walls scarcely able to support their new roofs of thatch. Out of one of these buildings a dark uncouth man was carrying a milking pail. He stared after them with something of the air of a savage watchdog on a chain. They hurried on and came at last to what was evidently the front door, on the opposite side of the house to their camp. It seemed as though this and the entrance hall on to which it opened and been rebuilt or refaced at some later date, though one still remote in time. The great door was approached by a flight of massive stone steps up which Dominic and Josephine climbed, their minds a little uneasy as to the kind of welcome that might be waiting for them at the other side of that great nail-studded oak door. Dominic had to stand on tiptoe to reach the knocker, and the sound seemed to reverberate through a dozen great rooms at once. Then there was silence.

From somewhere far inside the house the tune of talking made itself heard; a man's low voice talking to himself, perhaps, since no one answered it. But two pairs of footsteps, light and firm, were heard approaching. Then the door was flung open and a tall man appeared, the master of the house, no doubt.

He was young and strong and ruddy; a farmer perhaps, sun-tanned in his bare-armed open-necked shirt, but he wore the grace of a smile on his friendly face. Beside him stood a young woman, matching him in height, wearing no shoes on her feet nor hair-pins in her long jet-black hair, which surrounded a face both grave and shapely and fell down over the black shawl on her shoulders. They looked the children up and down without speaking.

Dominic led off. "If you please, sir, can we buy some eggs here?"

"And where do you come from at all?" asked the master of the house.

"We're camping down by the river," Dominic answered.

"We hope you don't mind," put in Josephine hastily. "We'll be very careful about broken bottles and . . . er . . . fires," she added, trying not to think of the one they had left behind blazing so cheerfully by itself.

"Sure, you can stay there the night," said the young man at once. "As for the eggs. . . ." He looked towards his companion. Silently she turned and vanished into the interior of the house, returning almost immediately with six eggs in a bag, a jug of milk and a small jar of honey. At the children's thanks she smiled gravely and remained looking from one to the other.

" 'Twill be wet tonight, I'm thinking," the man said then. "Ye can tell your dad that if he's troubled keeping the weather out, ye can come up here and welcome. By the Saints, there's room for all in Port Castle, however many ye be!"

"Oh thank you, sir," said Dominic and Josephine together. "We . . . er . . . won't forget to tell him," Dominic added. "And how much is it for the eggs and honey and milk?"

"I'll tell you tomorrow when you bring back the jug," said the man, and the two of them turned back into the house, the young woman still looking over her shoulder at the children.

They did not drink the milk. It was cows' milk and, remembering their promise to their parents, they poured it away scrupulously, to the last drop. Dominic said it was an oblation to the spirits of the home. Josephine said it was rather a waste but she supposed they'd better. But there was enough goats' milk left in the lemonade bottle for their tea, still leaving some for tomorrow's breakfast, and they made a good meal off scrambled eggs followed by thick slices of bread and honey. Then they sat down together at the door of their tent and watched the sun dipping slowly behind the house. Soon, very tired, they rolled themselves in their blankets and lay down where they were. It seemed too beautiful an evening to leave behind.

"Did you hear what he called the house?" said Josephine. They talked in low voices though they could not have said why.

"Port Castle," Dominic answered. "It did look rather grand, didn't it—I mean, once?"

"I'm glad they're so near," said Josephine. "I liked them, didn't you?"

"Yes, they were nice," Dominic agreed. "Nice, but queer. Funny how she left him to do all the talking. Do you think she was dumb?"

"Dumb, or just shy?"

"But she couldn't be shy of us," he argued.

"I don't know. Suppose you lived in that house where everything echoes, and never saw any children, and had nobody but him and the cows to talk to. . . ."

"And that angry-looking cowman," put in Dominic.

"And yet, you know," Josephine meditated; "he was rather like her in a way. They seemed to belong to the same world, except that she was beautiful and he was . . . almost deformed."

"And both of them were queer; I know what you mean," said Dominic. "Did you see the way she looked at us?"

"Yes, that's just what I mean," his twin agreed.

"It's very quiet here," Dominic continued. "I don't think I've ever been anywhere so quiet before. Supposing it makes us dumb too?"

Josephine laughed softly. "But I like it, don't you?"

THE START

Suddenly they heard a voice in the stillness. Not a human voice; in fact it came from a donkey from across the river, braying as though he would split his vocal cords. They were startled at first and then laughed with relief. "It will seem less lonely now," said Josephine.

"I seem to remember," said Dominic, "Jim Lyons saying once . . . that a donkey braying . . . was a sign of. . . ."

But Josephine was asleep.

CHAPTER VI

Echoes in Port Castle

Rain. It came pattering down in great drops on the leaves of the old oak tree beneath which they lay, and when the drops had joined other drops they ran off the leaves in tiny streams on to the children's startled faces. By the time they had remembered why rain should be falling upon their faces, they were getting quite wet.

"Well, there's the tent," said Dominic. "We'd better get inside it."

And, not stopping to unroll their blankets, they wriggled backwards into the tent.

But the rain was not all that the night had brought. There was a rumble in the air for a few seconds longer, and after it had ceased there came a dazzling flash, followed almost immediately by a crack so deafening that the two children sprang into something as near a sitting posture as the height of their tent permitted.

"Let's go into the house," Josephine urged, and by the light of the next flash Dominic thought how wide and black her eyes had grown.

"Are you frightened?" he asked. "I thought you didn't mind thunderstorms?"

"It depends where I am!" Josephine defended herself. "Have you forgotten we're underneath an oak tree? And your voice sounds rather shaky too!"

But in the darkness another noise was making itself heard;

a steady stammer of drops falling upon a metallic something.

"I believe the tent is leaking," said Dominic. "I noticed when I was putting it up a lot of tiny holes in one corner, as if the mice had made a nest there, and now the rain is coming through on to the kettle!"

"Let's go up to the house," Josephine repeated. "They did ask us, didn't they?" And this time he felt it would be cruel not to let her go.

"Won't they all be asleep?" he said, but he was reaching for the painted mackintosh. Josephine snatched her blue school mack and, carrying their blankets and by the light of a troubled moon, they scurried up the path that led to Port Castle.

No, they were not all asleep. High up a candle burned, as though to light just such travellers as they. They got to the great door and turned the handle. It was unlocked. As they entered the door the light came down the stairs to meet them. It illumined a huge entrance hall, antlers making fantastic shadows on its ceiling, old portraits hanging on its high walls. From below it lit the beautiful face of the farmer's wife. It was animated, almost to the point of laughter. She beckoned to them and with her hand on her lip led the way through to a large room at the back of the house facing on to the courtyard and empty except for a row of shallow earthenware bowls ranged along a stone shelf. On the far side, in a large open hearth, a fire had been laid.

With never a word she knelt before it setting it alight, and soon the whole room from its tiled floor to its oak-beamed ceiling reflected the rosy glow of its flames. She took their blankets from them and hung them before it to dry, bringing in others and pillows for their heads. She piled more turf on the fire and then at last she seemed satisfied and with a smile and what might have been a word left them.

"Didn't she say something?" whispered Dominic.

"Yes, but what was it?" Josephine whispered back.

"Nothing that I could understand," said Dominic, and

with the riddle still unravelled, they laid their heads on their pillows and slept.

They awoke together to the sound of a strange singing at no great distance from where they lay. At first it was not much more than a quavering song that went up and down and on the upper notes, sung almost with a woman's voice, was decorated with many turns and trills. Then Dominic suddenly began to pay attention. Bright-eyed he listened, doubt turning to certainty and then back again to doubt. "It's almost . . ." he said. "Yes, I do believe it's the song Miley sang; the song of the Green-coated Boy!"

He and Josephine listened as though bound by a spell, trying to make words of the long-drawn-out syllables, the sighing melody which now and again seemed nothing more than the wind soughing in the trees, except that what might have been words, gave it a sort of rhythm. Dominic was on the point of stealing out to find where the song might have its origin when suddenly it ceased, they heard a stumbling footstep in the doorway and the uncouth man of whom they had yesterday caught a glimpse, blundered into the room, a brimming milk pail in each hand.

If he had looked angry before, this time he was evidently outraged. Resting his milk pails on the floor, he uttered a flow of language, incomprehensible to the children except that there was no mistaking its sense.

They tried to explain themselves. "We were *invited* in," Josephine tried.

"Invited?" he repeated as though there were no such word.

"Yes, by the hall door," Dominic added, pointing in that direction. "The farmer . . . the master . . . he said we could come."

"Adam?" the man uttered. Dominic, quite in the dark, nodded his head nevertheless and understanding seemed to be dawning between them.

Shaking his head, he gave a disapproving grunt and, without again looking in their direction, turned himself to

59

the work of transferring the milk in the pails into two of the large bowls that stood empty.

The children looked at that unfriendly back, torn between prudence and their burning curiosity. "That song that you were singing . . ." Dominic broke the silence at last. "I know it too."

The man looked at him dully, evidently still much offended. "Who taught it to you?" Dominic continued, speaking very slowly and clearly. "Was it the Green-coated Boy?"

This time the man looked up. He appeared to ask a question.

Dominic hummed the scrap of tune that he remembered.

Intelligence beamed suddenly in the outlandish face. Again his talk flowed, incomprehensible as before, but his cheek flushed, his eye darted from one to the other. One might almost say that he was smiling. Suddenly nodding with emphasis and seeming to be promising them something, he disappeared from the room. They waited. It would not have surprised them if he had reappeared as suddenly with the Green-coated Boy himself beside him. But his footsteps died away. They never saw him again.

CHAPTER VII

The Enchanted Island

The air was wonderfully clear next morning. To the children it seemed like an invitation to leave their snug beds and the still glowing turf on the hearth, to return to their tent, the canoe and the river that was to lead them in the way of their dreams. They slipped out by the door that their strange visitor had left open, ran down the path strewn with leaves and branches torn down in last night's storm, to find the river just beginning to show blue beneath great scarves of vapory white clouds which a northerly wind was whirling upwards and away.

They ate a quick cold breakfast and then, whilst Dominic was packing up the tent and loading the canoe, Josephine went back to the house with the milk jug and money to pay for the eggs. She would take one last look at the room which had sheltered them from the storm, with its fallen dignity and air of belonging to the past. For one night it had been theirs, and somewhere in the recesses of their brains, she thought, she and Dominic would carry its picture so long as memory remained. But already the fire had been put out, the magic was gone and the milk pails prevailed.

Then she saw the room already had an occupant. Adam's wife was kneeling in a far corner beside one of the bowls skimming the milk. At Josephine's entry she turned, and Josephine approached her holding out a shilling, and saying very clearly in case she was deaf as well as dumb, "For the eggs."

The woman looked at it uncomprehendingly and then her face lit with a smile.

"No," she said, shaking her head vigorously, and then "No!" again, as though it were the only word she knew. Then she went to another room and returned with a bagful of little apples, crimson and gold, which she put into Josephine's hands and, going to the door with her, uttered a word which must have meant good-bye, for she waved her hand and smiled again.

"She's not dumb after all!" Josephine brought the news as she raced to what had been their camp a few moments later. "She said 'No' twice when I offered her the money, and another word that I couldn't understand just as I was going. And look what she's given us!"

"Then it was probably the Irish for either 'Good-bye' or 'Apples'," said Dominic, taking one and beginning to munch it. "Do you know, I thought of that as the answer whilst you were up there. She and her brother—I think he must be her brother, don't you?—are Irish-speaking. Adam must have picked them up somewhere in the West and he being of these parts is English-speaking. Poor woman, no wonder she's quiet! How long do you suppose it will take her to learn something besides 'No'?"

"But she must have learnt 'Yes'," Josephine reminded him, "because if she hadn't—don't you see?—she wouldn't have been here!"

Dominic was kind enough to chuckle at his sister's sagacity as he held the boat for her to get in. He promised her that on the following day she should have the place of honor, set the pace and act as steersman in the bows. Dominic was a man of honor and it was not his fault if he did not keep his promise.

Very soon the river widened into a little lough, the water became choppy although the wind, now behind them, had dropped to the softest breath. But it was exhilarating to feel the punch of the waves on their thighs through the thin skin of the boat. Now they noticed buoys, some red and some black, up on their course and it became evident that two separate channels had been marked. They took the black right-hand one as that way seemed to take the straightest course down the Shannon. Just before the lough narrowed again into a river, they came upon a little bay which seemed a paradise for picnickers. It had a tiny harbor almost entirely enclosed, with sweet herbs and wild flowers, scabious, wild peppermint and Grass of Parnassus growing on its brink, and grey rocks inviting a landing on its firm green turf. The lough stretched its blue and silver mirror beneath a sky that was now a cloudless blue and far away, not yet left quite behind, Slieve Anierin rose, a lilac cone, into the paler sky of the horizon. If he appeared to them in the light of a friendly old guardian as they gazed at him a little wistfully, their minds were untroubled by the future, their only fear that of being pursued and brought back before they reached Ulphin, and even that chance seemed to them remote, for no one had known what was in their minds and fortunately, as Dominic said, rivers carry no tracks.

They sun-bathed in that limpid sun-warmed water till hunger drove them ashore for a meal. This time they boiled two of the Port Castle eggs and then made some weak tea in the egg water which they drank with plenty of sugar but no milk. "When we come to a village with a shop in it, let's buy some ginger pop," Dominic suggested.

"Yes, and a tin of Nestlé's," Josephine added. "We've still got three and ninepence."

But before they came to any village, they had an unpleasant surprise. They found their way barred by a lock; barred indeed for it was a lock with no lock-keeper, it seemed, the banks too high to give any hope of success in carrying the canoe round to the other side.

But Dominic landed to explore a scent of flowers on the high bank and there, among the flowers and his grandchildren, the lock-keeper was found.

With delighted excitement, the grandchildren arose to see the canoe through the lock, a delight slightly marred by doubt on the old man's part as to what Dominic and Josephine would be thinking of doing on the other side, how old they were, and whether their dad and their mam were aware of their present activities.

"Me God above," said the lock-keeper. " 'Tis not I would lose my sweat opening the gates to two travelling children the like of yourselves looking for trouble! I'd sooner save the Devil a journey. Do ye not know 'tis a shilling itself 'twill cost you to pass through my lock, and you with no more than one pence or two between you, I'll swear!"

With great dignity Dominic produced a shilling, which the lock-keeper took and examined closely, half-expecting it, it seemed, to unfold and reveal a chocolate drop.

"Open the lock, Grand'fer, open it now," cried the oldest of the grandchildren. "'Twill maybe sink a small little boat like that one, and we to see them drown!" And reluctantly the old man prepared to give way.

" 'Tis yous is the first ones through the lock in all the summer," cried the oldest grandchild to Dominic.

"They are not. There was the two young men with the dog in just such a boatie not many days since, and you in your beds," the old man rebuked them.

But having accepted them as passengers, he was scrupulous to give them all the help and advice they needed; it was an enormous lock and they had reason to feel gratitude before the formidable passage was made and themselves afloat again, their dues paid, on the still upper waters.

Since their picnic, which should have revived them, their arms had seemed to flag, the water to be less buoyant, the boat curiously heavier. This condition increased as time went on, and at Cootehall, the village they reached soon after, the need for ginger pop seeming to outweigh all other considerations, they went ashore and down the long village street till they found at last a store with a row of the little stone bottles opposite the bar, of which they bought a bottle each, as Nestlé's milk proved beyond their now diminished means. In fact, when they counted over the money in Dominic's pocket, they found that only one and threepence remained.

"We must get on," Dominic said. "If we aren't careful, we shall run out of money before we ever get there!"

They were sitting tied up near the bridge, drinking in tiny sips so that the ginger pop should last as long as possible. Josephine looked at her twin thinking that for the first time he looked tired as well as anxious.

"We've still got lots of food, and all those lovely apples," she said. "We mustn't spend any more on drink: just boil the river water instead."

"Well, hurry up and put that down," said Dominic. "There's still lots of time before sunset."

Josephine took a long breath and swallowed the rest of the ginger pop and for some time afterwards the river resounded with her hiccups.

For perhaps a couple of miles more they struggled on, the sun dropping lower and lower, and then the river gave them another surprise. It opened out and suddenly a large lake's glassy surface was spread before them. Hardly a breath of wind came to stir the rushes. As their paddling ceased, there was no sound to take its place in the hushed air, only from the far distance a small quacking broke the stillness as a flight of wild duck came wheeling by in a great circle overhead. The children followed them with ears and eyes until at last the distance annihilated those small brown bodies and their ardent voices together.

"There are islands," said Dominic. "I wonder which way the river runs?"

Josephine's face fell. If they were to lose their way in this beautiful but baffling lake of many channels, for how much longer could she continue to paddle before they found their way back into the right one?

Dominic suddenly made up his mind. "I'm going to put you and the heavy bundle of tent ashore," he said, "and I'll explore the lake till I find the entrance at the other side. Perhaps I'll find a good camping-ground too."

She obeyed, too tired to argue, and for a while, seated on the bundle, watched the ever-diminishing outline of the canoe. Then abruptly, her attention wandering, it and Dominic disappeared altogether.

The lake seemed scarcely real to her, its loveliness unearthly, sinister even, as though she and Dominic were mortals strayed into some spot where mortals do not belong. The shore behind her seemed darkly buried in deep woods which gave no sign of life, human or otherwise. The lake's surface, rosy now under the light of evening, was broken only by little islands and their reflected watery counterfeits. Perhaps Dominic would choose to camp on one of them tonight. It would be an adventure after his own heart. After hers? She was less sure. She wished now that he would come back. It must be half an hour since he had been gone. She listened for the sound of his returning paddles, but was met only by that supernatural silence.

She thought of calling his name, of shouting, and then when he answered she would ask if he had found the way out of the lake. "Dominic," she called, and the fear in her own voice startled her. "Dominic!" Everything around her seemed to be listening intently, to be holding its breath to see what she would do if no answer came. Then she heard her own voice repeated very clearly from across the lake. "Dominic!" it called back; "Dominic!" Even more desperate than her own it sounded. She had to call again, only to still those echoes. "Dominic!" she shouted still more wildly, and the quavering sobbing echoes answered her again.

She hid her face, shuddering. There was a noise of soft wings. The ducks had returned. From up there they must know where Dominic had gone. The water must know; the dark woods too. Everything knew, excepting her alone.

Then out of the stillness Dominic's voice sounded in her ears, clear and immediately near, not even raised in a shout. "I've found a lovely camping-ground," it said, and then no more.

"Where?" she cried. "Dominic, where are you?" And the echo called back "Where?"

But that was all, and no amount of calling would bring

back another sound. Then indeed she felt there was something accursed in a place that played such freakish tricks with sound; which had an echo for her voice with which the islands rang again, but allowed his to fall away into silence.

At last there disentangled itself from the reflection of a shadowy cape the silver outline of the canoe. She sprang to her feet waving frantically and presently he was beside her.

It was difficult to believe that he had not heard her calling, or that some trick of sound had brought his voice to her once only, but so it was. Meanwhile he had discovered, he said, the prettiest camping-ground she had ever seen, on an island —"a magic island almost," he added. "Just wait and see! But there's some bad news too, I'm afraid."

Josephine thought that no news could be bad now that they could face it together. But she agreed that what he had to tell was serious enough. There was no river running out of the lake; nothing but a little stream that emptied itself into the opposite end, and they now understood why their day's paddling had proved so tiring. The current was slight, but it flowed the other way. "Look," Dominic added, and threw a bunch of grasses into the lake. Near its exit as they were, they could see the current gently, slowly bear the grasses away towards the river by which they had come.

"So all today's paddling goes for nothing," Dominic ended. "The shilling we spent at the lock and the one we shall spend tomorrow. We shall have to go the whole way back to where the red buoys marked the other channel. Oh, why wasn't there some one to tell us the way!"

"There was, but we wouldn't have understood them if they had," his sister reminded him. "And anyway, if we do have to go back, we shall have the current with us tomorrow."

Now as they paddled together round a bend of the shore, there rose before them an island that had borrowed from the evening mist some of the shimmering quality of a mirage. It was approached from the water by flat silvery grey rocks which made a landing easy. In the center, a green hill lifted steeply to a tree-crowned height and amongst the trees, which had a look of great antiquity, two grey old ruins stood, it might be of an abbey and a castle.

Though it was growing late, for some time after they landed they ran hither and thither upon this nameless island, unable to leave its vistas and its green glades till at last, the light beginning to fade, they applied themselves to the more serious tasks of setting up the tent, lighting a fire and cooking their supper. There were still two eggs left, and these they fried with bacon in the Major's little cooking-pot. Twilight was falling when the meal was ready at last, the picnic rug spread out upon the ground, two tin plates and mugs, a loaf of bread, some butter in a greasy packet, and a pot of jam were ranged ready upon it, and finally the kettle boiled. Dominic and Josephine, sitting on their haunches beside the rug, snuffing the eggs and bacon, felt they had never before understood the meaning of hunger.

Then something very strange happened. Before their eyes the loaf of bread began to move sideways, to sidle itself towards the edge of the rug. For a moment they watched it transfixed, then Dominic cried "Rats!" and now they both saw them, enormous grey rats, bold with hunger, gathering for the feast. Josephine felt sure she was going to be violently sick, but instead she found herself leaping to her feet beside Dominic and with shouts driving the grey things away into the shadows. But almost immediately they were back, and as the evening darkened, so the rats grew bolder and more insistent. The children had swallowed the eggs and bacon somehow between onslaughts made with their paddles in their hands, and now they began to wonder where they should put their food for the night. "We can't have it in our tent!" Josephine exclaimed, and Dominic agreed that they were not asking for that kind of trouble. In the end he had the idea of putting everything eatable in the center of the rug and hoisting it by a rope over the branch of a tree. And only then did the rats leave them.

But somehow, even for Dominic, the gilt was off the ginger-bread of this magic island of his, the enchantment was broken.

When later on four pretty black heifers approached from nowhere to watch them at their evening ablutions, they disliked them at sight and when they presently added their inquisitive trespassing to that of the rats, the children were furious. They were tired, and they wanted nothing so much as to be left in peace. The ever-renewed astonishment of the heifers at their doings exasperated them. Finally, quite worn out, they retreated to their tent for sleep, but even then Josephine was soon to be awakened by the sound of light steps tripping and stumbling about the guy-ropes, followed by sounds of Dominic blasphemously belaboring the visitors with a paddle. How many times she awoke during the night to that sound, she could never tell, any more than she could tell where her twin had learnt all the very impressive words he was using. She came at last to the conclusion that he was making them up.

The last time she awoke it was to hear his voice calling her. She put out her hand and touched his arm. "Why, you're wet," she said, still half-asleep. "Is it raining? Where's your mackintosh?"

"Over there on my blanket," he said. "I got tired of taking it off and putting it on again every time those horrible heifers came. It's been raining and now the wind's getting up. Can't you hear it?"

She listened. A new and ominous note had certainly been added to the voices of the night, the sound of the wind rising and rushing through the trees. "The waves are getting quite big," Dominic said. "We must get off while we can still launch the canoe."

She had a picture of herself and Dominic marooned on this island, perhaps for days, with only the hungry rats for company. She tumbled out of her blanket to help Dominic lower the tent, to find that in the intervals of Dominic's vigils, the black heifers had broken one of its poles, dunged on the Major's cooking stove and drunk up the one bucket of water they had been to the trouble of boiling the night before. But there was no time for lamentation. The rain was falling again and the waves rising, so, barely stopping to eat a hunk of bread apiece, they rolled up and stowed away the tent and damp bedding and launched out on to the rough waters glad of one thing only, to be quit for ever of this baleful island.

CHAPTER VIII

Fellow-Travellers

They launched out into the waves, Josephine gladly relinquishing her claim to the seat in the bows, and immediately Dominic said: "Paddle as hard as you can till we get back into the river. I'll do the steering."

Josephine paddled with all her might, but she was aware of the anxious part that was Dominic's, for whilst they were obliged to keep the canoe's bow head on to the waves for fear of capsizing, the entrance to the lake was on a line diagonal to the waves. She could feel the force he was putting into his paddling and tried to match her strength with his and at last, in spite of a contrary wind and the rain that lashed their faces, they entered thankfully the blessed haven of the river's banks.

It was only then that Josephine realized that Dominic's teeth were chattering loudly. As they waited a moment to regain breath, to rest their arms and backs, a glance as he turned his head told her that all was not well with her twin. In spite of flushed cheeks, his face had a grey pinched look and his hand as she touched it was shaking with cold.

"Dominic!" she cried, dismay in her tones, "are you ill?"

Dominic shook his head. "It's only my back," he said. "I think I've got rheumatism after getting wet in the night."

He was wearing the painted mackintosh but beneath it she remembered how wet his coat had felt to her touch.

"We must go somewhere where you can get warm and

71

dry," she said. "What about that village—Cootehall, wasn't it called?"

"I'm worried about the money," Dominic confessed. "How can we ask someone to let us come into their house and dry ourselves when all we have is one and threepence to give them?"

"Adam and his wife wouldn't take anything at all," Josephine protested warmly. "But it's such a long way to Port Castle and, oh dear, we'll have to go through that lock first and that will leave us with only threepence! Oh Dominic, do you think we shall often lose our way?"

But Dominic rallied her. "I'm all right, really," he said, and gave a rather crooked smile. "Let's get on to Cootehall, anyway, and buy a nice hot breakfast and then I daresay we shall both feel better, and perhaps Adam would ask his brother-in-law to tell us the way to Ulphin. It can't be far away really. We've come so far in these two days."

As he seemed determined to be cheerful, Josephine felt it would be out of place to remind him that one of those two days had not brought Ulphin any nearer but quite the reverse; an error that it would take another day to mend.

How they reached Cootehall Josephine never knew, for during much of those two miles she was paddling the canoe single-handed with only the slight current to help her, and against a wind that, whenever the river widened, beat up the water into small choppy waves, and itself did its best to turn the boat's bows to port or starboard whenever the wind's course and the river's did not agree.

At last the bridge that marked the village came in sight, and against the landing-stage beside it they found to their surprise a canoe like their own only newer and therefore, they were bound to admit, at least as handsome. And so at last the marionette had a fellow-traveller to wave to. Of the canoe's occupants there was no sign.

Thankfully they moored their boat beside the other. Then Josephine turned to her brother. "I'm going to find somewhere that will take us in," she said. "There's no need for us both to go. Look, wait for me inside that shed out of the wind and rain. I won't be away long. Is your head aching?"

"Just a bit," answered Dominic. He certainly looked very queer. She would not have been surprised if he had dropped asleep at any moment, so heavy were his eyes. She found an empty wooden case and made him sit on it; he sank down all in a bunch, his teeth still chattering. She took the one and threepence from him and set out to walk as fast as she could down the wide straight street that ran through the center of the village with more of fear than hope in her heart. At the first general store that she came to she asked them, could they please let a boy come in and dry his clothes and warm himself by the fire? "I'm afraid he's caught cold camping," said she, and showed her shilling.

"Holy Virgin, and would you wonder at it the rain we're having!" cried one of two girls in the back of the shop. "But it's no fire that we have here, nor any sticks dried for to make one. Faith, ye'd better try at Mulvaney's over yonder. They'll take him at Mulvaney's, sure, don't you think so, Nora?"

Nora was positive they would. But at Mulvaney's, which proved to be the shop where they had bought their ginger pop, though it was now after ten by the post office clock, they were not even awake. Josephine's desperate knockings brought at last a yawning lad to open the door, unshaven, his eyes glued with slumber. Him she sent with a pressing message to Mulvaney himself, begging him to come down and see her and discuss this urgent matter of a room with a fire for which, she added, he would be well paid.

But Mulvaney from the depths of his bedroom was adamant. He would come down to see nobody. And as for a room, why didn't she try Mrs. Donovan's at the end of the village? Sure, if anybody in Cootehall would take in a sick child, it would be Mrs. Donovan.

So to Mrs. Donovan's Josephine betook herself, "the very last house in the village," knowing well that if Mrs. Donovan didn't like the looks of her, there would be nothing for it but to push on somehow all the weary way back to Port Castle and throw themselves on the mercy of Adam's wife—if they ever got so far. She felt sure that there they would not be turned away. So she reflected as she waited for Mrs. Donovan to answer her faltering knock.

Mrs. Donovan opened her door with two little Donovans frolicking around her petticoats. "In the name of God," said she, "it's not anything that's catching the poor child is suffering from? Tell me now, has he a high temperature, and what like was his tongue this morning, and was there anything in the shape of a strawberry rash upon his chest? It's not I would bring a case of the scarlet fever to infect me poor children!"

"I want me long dress, Mam, to cover up me drawers!" wailed one of the poor children from the background.

Ignoring this request Mrs. Donovan listened carefully as Josephine outlined Dominic's history during the last twenty-four hours and at the end, with a heart evidently melted, "Ah, the poor bosthoon," she said. "There's quare things happening on they islands, and more than rats, they say, to be reckoned with at nights. Sure, I'll light the kitchen fire and hot him a drink. We'll dry his clothes too, and he can lie on the sofa there till he feels better. Bring him in quick now, out of the rain!"

Better news, Josephine felt, she could not have heard. Thanking Mrs. Donovan warmly, she ran out into the rain and was soon back at the river bank, peeping into the shed where she had left Dominic.

"It's all right, Dominic," she cried. "I've found. . . ." Then she stopped short. There was the empty case upon which she had left Dominic seated; there was the pool of water which had run off the painted mackintosh. But of Dominic himself there was not a trace. He had utterly vanished.

So the nightmare had begun again. Perhaps, she told herself, he had gone off for a walk in the hope of getting warm. She crossed the bridge and took the road away from the village, but no familiar figure in painted mackintosh was to be seen. She visited the first store she had been to in the vain hope that he might have followed her there, or to Mulvaney's, but Mulvaney's remained obdurately shut. She searched the river upstream and then down, but it was, as before, as though Dominic had never been. One thing she did see, however, just below the bridge on the river's bank, and that was a brown tent, far bigger than their own, from which came the hum of men's voices and at the flap of which a Scottish terrier was mounting guard.

Here at least were human beings who might have seen Dominic as he left the shed, and with a determined step, Josephine approached the tent and coughed.

The immediate result was that the dog leapt to his feet with a growl and bit Josephine's shoe. But what followed was of so miraculous a nature that the Scottie might well have been her guardian angel in ingenious disguise. For two tousled heads were thrust out of the tent opening to call him in, and Josephine immediately stepped forward.

"If you please, sir," she said to the nearest head, "I have lost my brother."

Consternation descended upon the faces opposite. "My dear child," replied the owner of the head, "I am truly sorry to hear it. Is there any way in which we can help you?"

"Have they held the inquest yet?" suggested the other. "Is it for that you want us?"

"Oh *no*!" Josephine recoiled. "He's ill—very ill perhaps, but not dead!"

"Then where is he?" asked Number One, who seemed to be the talker of the two. "Can we go and see him? We might be able to help."

"Where he is is what I hoped you would tell me," Josephine answered, touched and surprised at their immediate interest in her twin. "You see, I left him sitting in a shed down by the bridge, and when I came back, he had gone! I've been looking for him for ever so long."

"Was he wearing a mackintosh," asked the talkative one, "and carrying a largish bundle?"

"Yes, with a painted sleeve—at least the mackintosh had."

"Then there was a boy with a mackintosh of the sort you describe went past here about half an hour ago. He was carrying a bundle, and he went round the side of that hill to the left."

"Then he's gone to put the tent up," cried Josephine seeing light at last. "I suppose as I didn't come back and he was so sleepy, he thought he'd put up the tent and go and lie down in it."

By this time the three of them were walking in the direction in which Josephine's new friends had watched Dominic disappear, and Josephine was tempted by their kindly sympathy to tell them of Dominic's illness and of her anxiety for him. "Do you think," she asked them, "there would be a doctor in this village who would come and see what is the matter with him? Though I'm afraid," she added, "I haven't got any money to pay him with. Only one and threepence that I've promised to Mrs. Donovan."

She saw the two of them exchange glances. "If it's a doctor you want," said the talkative one, "you've come to the right shop. We're two doctors from Dublin." And they began at once asking after Dominic's symptoms. They were reassuring for they knew of no sinister outbreak in these parts. "But from what you say, it might be typhoid fever," they said, "or it might be diphtheria, or again it might be nothing but a plain chill."

They had now arrived at a little hollow under the hill where, sure enough, they found the green tent erected and beneath it, Dominic asleep.

"Hm," said the quiet doctor, looking at him carefully. "The first thing is to find him a bed and to get him into it as quickly as possible."

Josephine hastened to explain that, if not a bed, a sofa by the fire had already been found and was awaiting the arrival of Dominic. The boy was now awakened and had the situation explained to him, Dominic listening with goggling eyes whilst Josephine related the finding not only of a sick-bed but of two doctors from Dublin to attend it. "I believe they're specialists," she whispered. "They seem to know the names of so many diseases, but they think yours is most likely only a chill."

It was decided that Dominic and Josephine should go at once to Mrs. Donovan's and get him in front of that fire whilst the two doctors packed up the dripping tent and followed them. They arrived at Mrs. Donovan's door simultaneously.

They found that excellent woman happy in the sense of good deeds accomplished. For in Josephine's absence she had decided to set up a small bed in a little room next to the kitchen where she had lit a fire on which the hot drink she had promised was already brewing.

"It's glad I am to see your dad and your uncle as well," she added, including the two doctors in her smiling greeting, evidently feeling that things were now on a more sound financial footing.

The two doctors exchanged glances which, however, resulted in nothing more than a wink.

"But 'tis a hard thing surely," she continued, "that I have no room fit to offer two gentlemen the likes of yourselves, and you to have to go out and leave a sick child behind you."

But the doctors explained that it was a thing that happened to them nearly every day. They would not think of troubling Mrs. Donovan at all, and would be round to settle with her in the morning for all the trouble she had already taken. And when they had done looking at the boy, they would return to their own tent by the river-side. They asked her to see to it that the children had as good a meal as they needed that evening, and kind Mrs. Donovan promised that she would do her all and utmost.

"The girleen can sleep on the sofa in the kitchen," she added. "We'll leave the door open between them and neither of them will feel strange so."

By this time Dominic, dressed in his clean shirt in a bed soft with the luxury of sheets, was ready in the next room to receive a professional visit. One of the young doctors, whose bedside manner can have had few rivals in all Dublin, soon had him galvanized into life and even laughter with his pleasant wit, whilst the other, whom his companion described as "the expert on diagnosis," regarded him from the foot of the bed quietly, rather shyly, but with a manner inspiring the maximum of confidence. The result of the consultation was that, although typhoid was not wholly ruled out yet, the probability was that "the boy is suffering from nothing but a plain chill."

They had intended, they said, out of all patience with the weather, to end their holiday that very day in the comfort of an hotel in Donegal, but now they had decided to stay on at Cootehall for another day, and would be round after breakfast tomorrow morning to take another look at their patient.

Dominic, indifferent to food, slept the rest of the afternoon and evening away. Josephine, too, was glad to creep to rest on the kitchen sofa, after doing full justice to a meal of scrambled eggs and bacon, eaten in the moon-eyed company of the two little Donovans.

CHAPTER IX

Sister Philomena

I n the morning, for all it was late summer, it was just as though spring had come back. From her bed on the sofa Josephine watched soft April showers alternate with a timid sun as soft. There was even a bird singing, and presently Dominic awoke, as bright a bird as any and very interested in what there might be for breakfast. When Mrs. Donovan put her head round the door to ask if an egg would be to his fancy, "Make it two!" was his immediate reply.

"Me sowl! hearken at him!" said Mrs. Donovan to Josephine. "A boy who can eat double eggs for breakfast is ready to break up the world!"

As soon as breakfast was over, as good as their promise, Dublin's two doctors appeared and pronounced themselves well pleased with the condition of their patient. There was no doubt that the plain chill was the right answer today. "But you may recollect," the Bedside Manner reminded them, "when Mrs. Donovan mistook us for your parents and guardians yesterday, we didn't give you away; today you don't get away with it so easily. Suppose you tell us now where your real parents are?"

"On the Gold Coast," Dominic answered glibly and flashed a look of triumph across to Josephine. There was a moment's pause.

"Then who is it you're running away from now?" was the next question, posed by the Specialist in Diagnosis.

"Our guardian," answered Josephine, her manner a little guarded.

"And where does he live?" asked the Bedside Manner.

Dominic became playful. "Up the river and over the hill," he replied.

Both doctors assumed a more serious air. "You realize," said the Diagnosis Specialist, "that as your medical practitioners, called in by one of you, we have full rights over your actions. Now do you think," he turned to Josephine, "it would be right for your brother, just getting over a sharp attack of fever—for I've rarely felt a hotter head than his was yesterday—to go back to the river after all the rain there has been, and is going to be"—he glanced out of the window—"and sleep in a damp blanket in that soaking tent?"

Josephine's defenses broke down. She realized it was exactly what she had been thinking herself for the past twenty-four hours. But it was cruel of him to wring such a confession from her. She looked at him fearfully and he returned her regard unsmilingly.

Dominic was looking at her too, but she tried not to meet his eyes. "Oh, Dominic," she cried in an agony of indecision, "we'd better tell them. There's all our money gone, and look, it's raining again!"

It was indeed. Heavily, obdurately, dashing all their hopes. In that downpour Ulphin seemed very far away, a dream dissolved in banks of cloud. The children let themselves be persuaded. Their two friends were ready with a plan. They had already found a man, one Charlie Halvey, who was prepared to convey them and their canoe on his asses' cart to Carrick-on-Shannon where there was a hospital, and in that hospital a Reverend Mother with whom the Bedside Manner was well acquainted. "She's a dear woman; you'll both love her," he said. "One night being well looked after in the convent will set you both up, and I'll write to your uncle, or maybe send him a telegram to tell him you're coming home in the Athlone bus tomorrow."

"And our canoe?" queried Dominic. "What will become of her?"

"The Reverend Mother," said the doctor, "has a very soft spot in her heart for all small things, children and canoes. You will find, I think, that she knows the very place where it can be left safely till you're able to send and fetch it home. I'll write a letter that you can give her, saying she's to take special care of the canoe."

So it was agreed, and even Dominic seemed to have resigned himself to the inevitable, though he had grown suddenly silent and his eyes, thought Josephine who knew him, had taken on a dreamy far-away look. Not quite so far away as Ulphin, she hoped.

Charlie Halvey was to fetch them in the afternoon, and it was to be a longish drive to Carrick, but they should be there by tea-time.

The Bedside Manner scribbled a note on Mrs. Donovan's writing paper to Reverend Mother which he gave into the care of Dominic and then, after an interview with Mrs. Donovan which seemed to leave their kind landlady entirely happy, the two doctors took an affectionate farewell of the twins, admonishing them to take warning by this holiday next time they thought of running away from home.

They then departed to send their telegram to Uncle Theo, and Dominic in the long drive in Charlie Halvey's cart took a malicious delight in tormenting Josephine by inventing comments made by that worthy man on receiving the news.

Perhaps it was the first time that a canoe with a marionette for figure-head had drawn up at the convent door. Heads of all sorts were soon bobbing at every window; old heads, young heads, sick heads and well heads and heads wearing the nun's veil.

Reverend Mother herself came down to see what chance could have brought this strange equipage to her door.

Whilst Dominic told her about the canoe, Josephine told her about Dominic, and Reverend Mother's kind face puckered with bewilderment as she looked from one to the other.

"Here's one telling me that his sister needs a lot of care, and the other that 'tis her brother that has had two doctors in charge of him. Who is it now that's the great invalid, for we've a bed in the children's ward just yawning for a smart boy like yourself, or is it the girl who has first claim?"

"Will she be quite safe here?" Dominic was inquiring, pouring out his anxieties in one of Reverend Mother's ears. "The least little kick, or putting her down on something sharp. . . ."

"My dear child, in this hospital . . ." began Reverend Mother.

"But last night his temperature was *very* high," Josephine was insisting to the other ear. "The doctor who is so good at diagnosis quite thought it might be typhoid fever."

"I'm afraid she's very fragile," continued Dominic, perceiving his advantage and making the most of it. "Nothing but a bit of skin dragged over a few bones."

"Dominic, what a tease you are!" cried Josephine, now thoroughly disconcerted by the searching looks which Reverend Mother was bestowing upon her. "Why don't you give her the letter?"

"Ah, the letter! I was nearly forgetting the letter," exclaimed Dominic, summoning his most innocent look. And to Josephine's great relief he at last took the letter from his pocket and handed it to Reverend Mother.

"Och, the dear lad!" was Reverend Mother's first exclamation and one which in Dominic's view showed great generosity, all things considered, until he realized it was to the Bedside Manner that it referred. "The doctor is a very old friend at this convent," Reverend Mother continued, "and any friend of his is sure of a welcome from all of us, and their canoe as well." She laughed. "And how should I know," she went on, "it was a canoe you were telling me of, when I thought 'twas your sister with the delicate complexion. . . ."

"Skin," put in Dominic.

"And the fragile limbs. . . ."

"Bones," Dominic corrected.

"Heaven help the child for he's nothing but a wilful deceiver," laughed Reverend Mother. "But we don't bear malice here. Send me Sister Philomena," she called to a young novice who was passing through the hall. "Ask her can she spare me half an hour of her time?"

Almost immediately Sister Philomena's step was heard approaching the doorway and the next moment Sister Philomena herself, young, gentle, and yet with an eye that sparkled softly, stood before them, looking inquiringly at Reverend Mother and from her still more inquiringly to Dominic and from Dominic to Josephine. By those two glances both children were subdued. Thereafter they accepted Sister Philomena as their friend.

"Take these two children to the bathroom," said Reverend Mother, "and see that they each have as deep and as hot a bath as the water will allow, and with plenty of soap handy too. Make up two beds in the small visitors' rooms and see that they have something clean to sleep in, and then come to me again."

They followed Sister Philomena up the stairs, a little abashed at the stir which it seemed their arrival had provoked in this place of hushed dignity and calm. But there was nothing in Sister Philomena's manner to suggest that they were anything but honorable and esteemed guests as she left them in two little adjoining bedrooms telling them that she would return when their baths were ready. And return she did, with a little pile of clean things for each of them: pink flannel pyjamas for Dominic; pink flannel nightgown for Josephine.

"What have you in your bundle?" she asked her, "for if you've nothing cleaner than what you have on, you'll have to stay in the hospital pink nightwear till I have your own clothes washed and ironed."

But from this ignominy their spare clothes saved them, and

before long, bathed and dressed, combed and brushed, they were awaiting Sister Philomena's return.

She made a great play of astonishment at the improved picture they now presented. "The lovely children you are!" she cried. "Who would have thought two such handsome children could have hidden beneath all the grime of those camping days!"

Josephine was rather offended. "But we always washed ourselves at night," she protested.

"And here you will wash in the mornings as well," put in Sister Philomena.

"*You* wouldn't have washed with a crowd of grey rats sitting round you in a ring," Dominic remonstrated.

"Rats, is it?" cried Sister Philomena. "And dear knows what might not have happened to two lone children like you! But come on, now; tell me all your terrible tales later. There's a great tea ready for you in the housekeeper's room and though I don't suppose you're hungry after all the fine picnics you've had out there in the boat, you must eat your fill or Reverend Mother will murder me!"

When they saw the meal that was waiting in the housekeeper's room, compounded of all the best things that Rectory children eat for breakfast, tea and supper, they said not another word but fell silently to work upon it whilst Sister Philomena filled and refilled their cups and plates as though there were nothing exceptional in children who turned up in an asses' cart with a canoe and ate three meals in one.

"Tell me now," she said as their appetites at last began to flag. "What sort of man is he, this uncle you've run away from?"

The children exchanged glances. What a lot Sister Philomena seemed to know! Should they treat her indeed as a friend?

"He's always reading old books written in Irish," said Dominic.

"So he doesn't talk to us much," added Josephine.

"Ah no, he wouldn't," was Sister Philomena's comment. "It's a hell of a language." She looked over her shoulder, but the housekeeper's door was shut. "It's no marvel it's soured the poor man is. Is there nobody else?"

"There's Nellie," Josephine answered. "She's his cook. We like her."

"But she's so taken up with Jim Lyons and whether the marriage is coming off," Dominic put in, "that she often doesn't notice if we're there or not."

"Indeed she must be distracted by such a doubt," answered Sister Philomena, her eyes filled with concern. "Say no more about her. Ye'll get no help from that one. Is there no one else at all?"

"Only our goat," answered Josephine sadly, "and she ought to have a husband too."

"We're looking for one now," added Dominic, finally unbending in the atmosphere of this confidential talk.

"But never now, on this river, in your canoe?" cried Sister Philomena becoming more and more intrigued by this narrative.

"Have you ever heard of a place called Ulphin?" Josephine asked almost in a whisper, with a glance too at the housekeeper's door.

"Indeed no, and what sort of a place is that?" asked Sister Philomena, her voice, too, catching their conspiratorial tones.

"Or do you know anything about the Green-coated Boy?" Dominic questioned her.

For a moment Sister Philomena said nothing and a puzzled look came over her face.

"Wait now," she said then, "was there not something about a song which that one had made?" She broke off, her eyes focused on some distant point as she struggled to reconstruct a memory that eluded her. The children looked at her, not daring to interrupt that searching mind. She came back to them.

"There was a woman a while back," she began, "came in here for her blindness, which she said was growing more

86

complete. A beautiful woman she was; not young though, you understand; a travelling woman, only not a tinker, and she came of a family that I'd heard of as a child, that travels in a caravan between Athlone and the West, where they belong. Hogan is the name, and some sort of hereditary blindness afflicts all the family. This woman, Kathleen Hogan, came here to have the opportunity to see the great eye doctor that comes up from Athlone. There was an operation on one of the eyes; the grafting of a cornea, but you wouldn't know about that. When she left us it seemed that she might see again after all, but she was to come back in three months' time and have the doctor look at her again."

"Yes, but the Green-coated Boy?" asked Dominic, "what did she tell you about him?"

"Whisht with you, I'm coming to that now. She was a musician herself, do you see; a famous harpist, so we were told, for of course there was no chance of finding out such a thing here. But she had a number of songs. . . . Oh, if you'd started her singing yesterday she could have carried on with her songs till the day after tomorrow, I do believe, without stopping once!"

"And the Green-coated Boy," Dominic urged, determined to bring her to it at last. "What did she tell you about him?"

"Ah, there you are! 'The Green-coated Boy' was the name of one of the songs she sang. No, that's not right. It was he that had taught her the song, though I don't know that it was he himself that had made it. I rather think she said the song was a very old one and was written in Irish as well as in English. Maybe that clever uncle of yours would know all about it."

This was a startling thought. Dominic and Josephine tried to accustom themselves to the thought of an Uncle Theodore actually linked with the Green-coated Boy.

"Was the song about Ulphin?" asked Josephine, feeling the suspense to be something more than she could bear.

"It was about a strange and beautiful country," answered

87

Sister Philomena, "but I cannot remember what was the name in the song. Wait now till I can call it to mind."

Dominic too was frowning in the effort of remembering. "Was it," he asked, "about

A land of beauty, a land of truth,
Where youth shall never grow old or pine."

Sister Philomena hesitated. "Maybe it was, but those words I cannot remember. It was something like this:

Come back to me, lady, to love and to shine
In the land that was thine in the long ago . . .

And there was some more about 'hair of primrose hue, and the bloom of a cheek where the foxglove glows.' But it's the way it was, so soon as ever she started up that song, you could see all the old women in the ward begin to forget their aches and their pains, their grumbling and their quarrelling —and there's wars in that ward, I'm telling you, would turn a saint into despair! And they'd lay down quiet on their pillows and the smiles would come out at her song in place of the angry looks, and when she stopped singing and they began again to talk, it was of their homes that they spoke, or the good man they'd lost, or of their little grandchildren, or of the old cat maybe that was waiting for them at the corner of the fire."

Dominic too was leaning back with the sigh, it might be, of one who has found his way at last to a long-lost home. Only Josephine was far from satisfied.

"Was there nothing," she asked wistfully, "about a herd of wonderful black goats?"

Sister Philomena shook her head.

"You see," Josephine explained, feeling that things were getting a little out of proportion, "the real reason why we started out on this complicated journey was to find a husband for our nanny-goat. She's a very special goat, and at Ulphin there's a very special breed of black goats. There's one, 'a veritable Prince of Pucks,' they call him, and we were going to see if they would lend him to us for a time for a husband for our nanny, only . . . only, you see, we could never find Ulphin."

"Only," put in Dominic, "now we've found someone else who knows someone who knows the Green-coated Boy, it all sounds as if it's true and real again, and somehow, I don't mind so much even if we never find Ulphin at all." He paused as though deliberately bringing something to an end, and then:

"Now wouldn't you," he continued, giving Sister Philomena one of his sweetest smiles, "like to come and see our canoe? Do you know where they put her?"

"Of course I must see the canoe," cried Sister Philomena at once, "and I think I even know where to look for it, for I heard Reverend Mother tell the man who brought you here to drive it down to the river and leave it on the bit of land close to the Yacht Club boat-house. If you've really finished your teas, let's go down there now so that you can satisfy yourselves that she's perfectly safe."

She piloted them through the convent grounds where groups of patients, sitting or standing around in twos and threes enjoying an amicable chat, suddenly broke off their conversation to follow them with the same astonished eyes that had watched their arrival. There, close to the bank, under the shade of several large willows, the children saw the silvery form of their canoe. In the failing day Josephine was almost certain that as they approached a certain familiar figure in the bows lifted its arms in a salute, but she thought it best not to mention this to Dominic. He would have said it was only the wind. And besides, Dominic was busy cate-chizing Sister Philomena.

"Are you sure," he was saying, "she will be safe here till we can come and fetch her back? Are you certain there aren't any children at the convent who'll want to jump about in her or take her out on the river?"

"There now, isn't it a jealous old sea-captain that you are!" cried Sister Philomena. "Will I promise to come and look at her each day, and will you be easy then in your mind? If I tell you there's never a creature in the children's ward just now, and there's not one of those poor old cripples up yonder would risk their lives stepping into a thing like that, will that satisfy you?"

It had to, but you could see that the parting was a hard one for Dominic, whilst Josephine and the marionette had things to say to each other that were affecting them both. However, Sister Philomena had to hurry back for she would be on duty, she said, in ten minutes' time, but if they liked, they could come and talk to her before their bedtime whilst she was getting their clothes ironed and aired.

"You'll be off in the bus for Athlone with Sister Aloysia tomorrow morning," she told them, "and from there you can get another bus that takes you to Druim, near to where your uncle lives. He'll be there to meet you, Reverend Mother told me to tell you, for she's written him by this afternoon's post to tell him when the bus gets in. And don't let me ever hear of you making such a breakaway from the poor old man again. He must be nearly killed with all the worry of it, and your parents away."

"Who is Sister Aloysia?" asked Dominic.

"Why can't it be you that takes us to Athlone?" asked Josephine almost simultaneously, returning to the only part of the conversation that they intended to discuss.

"Because it's Sister Aloysia's day for visiting her old aunt in Athlone," Sister Philomena returned, "and tomorrow I shall be on duty all morning. But as it's a long journey you'll be making, I'll do this for you. I will put you up such a packet of sandwiches that you'll be the most of the day eating them and as you eat, you may think of Sister Philomena's words, for it's a poor lot of attention you are paying to them now."

"What queer places we seem to sleep in nowadays," said Josephine to Dominic as they conversed through half-open doors that night. "There was Port Castle in a thunderstorm, and then that horrible island with the rats and heifers. . . ."

"And last night at Mrs. Donovan's being a patient for two doctors, and tonight a convent that's a hospital as well," continued Dominic.

"And tomorrow night, back again with Uncle Theo and Nellie," finished Josephine. "I say, Dominic, do you think Uncle Theo will be very angry with us?"

"I'm perfectly certain he will," answered Dominic curtly, and said no more.

CHAPTER X

Sister Aloysia

At eleven o'clock the next morning the two children were following Sister Aloysia along the road that led to the stopping place of the bus for Athlone. Sister Philomena had been allowed to give them their breakfast in the housekeeper's room, and now they had bidden her a sorrowful farewell at the convent door.

"Promise me you'll be good children and do everything that Sister Aloysia tells you," Sister Philomena had said, and Josephine had promised.

"Are you sure you can't come with us instead of . . . her?" she had whispered, but the nun shook her head. For all answer she had put her finger to her lip and smiled.

But she had been as good as her word and each child now carried, as well as a well-aired blanket containing their spare clothes, nicely washed and ironed, a capacious packet of sandwiches. Their tent, dry at last though looking a little mouldy, they had carried back to the river bank when they went to say good-bye to the canoe.

"But it won't be for long," Josephine had assured the marionette. "We'll soon be sending to fetch you home, and then you'll stay with us always."

But Dominic's face was dark with apprehension. "Do you think so?" he asked. "Do you really think Uncle Theo will arrange to pay to have the canoe brought back, so that we can be off in her again? He'll never trust us now!"

Josephine turned a stricken face to her twin. "He wouldn't leave her here!" she cried. "Our own canoe? Oh, Dominic, he couldn't!"

"Couldn't he!" Dominic said, and his face was somber.

So it was with heavy hearts that they set out on this day that was to bring their travels to an end. For them no triumphant return with a Prince of Pucks for Amalthea. They were turning their backs on Ulphin. They were going back to be the Rectory children again.

But Sister Aloysia had reached the bus stop and was waiting for them to join her.

Sister Aloysia was not young like Sister Philomena, nor had she been as blessed with beauty. She had a double chin, a sharp red nose that poked itself inquiringly out of a face that bore an expression of bewilderment at the folly of others. There had been much talk of these children in the women's ward, and now, she felt, was her chance to bring back a tale that was assured of a good hearing and need lose nothing in the telling.

"How came your uncle," she began, "to buy you a dangerous boat the like of that one for a plaything? Sure, 'tis a miracle of God the both of you are not corpses floating on the river!"

Dominic turned to her coolly, summing her up. Josephine waited with resignation for the row that she knew would presently come.

"My uncle," Dominic began, "did not buy us the canoe. We bought her with our own money."

"Mercy on us, and where would two children the like of yourselves have found a sum of money sufficient to buy such a thing?" inquired Sister Aloysia, suspicion beginning to sow itself in her mind.

"In the pocket of an old mackintosh," returned Dominic in airy tones. "This mackintosh, as a matter of fact."

"Me God that I should listen to such a tale! And who put it there, do you ask me to believe?"

Dominic shrugged his shoulders. "The man the mackintosh belonged to, I suppose," he replied in a voice in which pity mingled with exasperation.

"So you stole the two of them together!" cried Sister Aloysia. "And you nothing but a common thief by your own telling! Little we guessed what a pair of vagabonds it was we was harboring! And Reverend Mother coming out to the kitchen herself to see if 'twas the best we had we was giving you! Oh, to think of two that we took for innocent children playing us such a trick!"

At this point Josephine felt it was time to intervene. "The man the mackintosh belonged to was dead," she explained, doing her best to make her voice sound very reassuring.

"Heaven help you! Is it murders too?" uttered Sister Aloysia almost in a scream. But presently, turning on Dominic a searching gaze, "But why," she added, "should I credit such a tale? The stain you have on your sleeve there is not red blood at all but green paint. And if 'tis after murdering a man you are, sure, we'd have the Gardai on your trail and 'twould be to prison you'd be going and not to your uncle's house at all. And you to be telling me such tales! Shame on your for a pair of liars, and so I shall tell Reverend Mother when I get back tomorrow."

But now, fortunately for Dominic and Josephine, there was a rumble and a stir and the Athlone bus had halted beside them.

It was market day in Athlone and the bus was nearly full. Near the front another nun was sitting and to the delight of the twins they saw Sister Aloysia push her way to an empty seat beside her and engage at once in an animated conversation the subject of which, to the two children sitting farther down the bus, was only too plain.

The bus started off and, the bus conductor coming round presently, Sister Aloysia called him to her and bought the tickets. Then, rustling and swaying down the bus, to their great surprise she put a ten-shilling note and several shillings into Dominic's hand.

"I'll stay to see you into the Druim bus at Athlone," she

said, "and not a moment longer, so ye'll have to pay for the next tickets yourselves. Here's the money over from what your kind friend sent Reverend Mother in his letter. It's two bad children ye are, and not deserving of any such kindness, but now, whisht with you, and let you not be crossing your tongues with any more lies!" And with a last withering look she returned to her seat.

The children looked at each other and then at the money in Dominic's hand.

"It's fourteen shillings and sixpence!" murmured Josephine in hushed tones.

"More than we had when we started," added Dominic, his eyes gleaming. "I say, Josephine!"

She looked at him expectantly but he said no more. After a while, a seat beside him becoming vacant, she slipped across. It was then she noticed that his eyes were shut.

She touched his shoulder with hers, indicating her presence, and he opened his syes. "I'm feeling sick," he said.

Josephine eyed him with concern. Neither of the twins could have been described as plump, but now, besides being thin, Dominic certainly had a drawn, travel-worn air and his twin remembered with a pang that it was only two nights ago that he had been in a high fever.

"It's because the bus is swaying so," she said. "Come and sit nearer the door and you'll feel better."

They moved down the bus to other vacant seats and soon after, the bus stopped for a woman and two children to alight.

Dominic's eyes were open and he was looking out of the window and along the road.

"Are you going to be sick?" Josephine asked him apprehensively.

"I thought I was going to be, but now I think I'm not," he replied and shut his eyes again as the bus moved on.

A short time afterwards, though no village or cross-road was in sight, the bus lumbered to a stop. The driver got out and lifted the bonnet. All conversation ceased; even Sister Aloysia up in front there was quiet, all attention focused on the movements of the driver, who now went to the other side of the bonnet, where the conductor joined him.

"Is it a puncture?" asked an anxious voice. "I have to be at my daughter's by half-twelve."

"No, I think 'tis the petrol running short," said another; "and no station now for another two miles or three!"

"But no, I think 'tis something gone in the insides," added a third. "I've noticed the coughs and splutters she was giving, the creature, more than a mile past."

This explanation was so satisfactory that on all sides conversation was resumed.

"Now I think I'm going to be sick," said Dominic quietly and hurried Josephine out of the bus, her face full of concern. "Behind that mound, quick!" he said, motioning with his head. "I don't want the whole bus looking on." He paused. "That awful old woman!" he said then. "Didn't it make *you* sick listening to her talk?"

"Well, you'd better be sick quickly," his twin urged, "or we shall be left behind."

But Dominic could not forget Sister Aloysia. "That old hen!" he said venomously. "Did you hear the way she was whispering and murmuring in the other nun's ear, with that fiendish grin on her face? Just to see the looks she was giving us as she told her tale made me want to throw up!"

"Well, please do it then and stop talking!" his sister implored him. "If the bus were to go on now, what would happen to us?"

"I'll be sick in a minute," Dominic promised, peeping out to see if the bus were moving. "Look at her now! You can see her chin wagging from here. 'I'm telling you this, I'm telling you that,' she's saying, 'and it's *bad* children they are!' "

At that moment there was a clanking of gears from the road, a rumble and a honk and Josephine from her side of the mound was just in time to see the bus accelerating. Desperately she climbed the mound, waving her arms in a frantic signal, but the bus seemed only to go the faster till before her eyes it disappeared over the brow of a hill. She turned those panic-stricken eyes on her brother and was amazed to see that he had remained perfectly calm.

"The bus has gone!" she cried, scarcely able to believe that he understood the full import of their dire predicament. He met her eyes unwaveringly, his own expressing nothing.

"I know it has. I saw it go," he said.

"Then what are we going to do?"

"I am going to find Ulphin," said Dominic.

She looked at him. She looked at the wide moorland stretched out to the empty horizon where some dark clouds seemed ominously to be piling themselves up against them, and she looked back at Dominic, his face pale and thin, with a flame burning in his eyes—a flame that turned to a twisted smile. Yes, there was something wonderful about Dominic; something quite beyond the reach of reason. She sighed, but she smiled too.

"Did you really feel sick in the bus?" she asked.

"Of course not, but how else could we have got away from that awful old woman?"

Then she noticed their bundles laying in the heather. "How did you manage to bring them without my seeing?" she asked.

"Easy enough, silly," he said tolerantly, "so long as I maneuvered you out first."

"And where are we going now?" she asked, feeling certain that he would know the answer already.

"Where do you suppose? Back to Carrick to fetch the canoe and then on down the river till we come to Ulphin. Look," he said, "we've got all Sister Philomena's sandwiches, and some of our own food as well. We've got plenty of money again; there's our tent and our canoe waiting for us. Why, we're better off than when we started! What are we waiting for?" And Dominic began to pick up the bundles.

Josephine had expected that they would return to the convent by the same route that the bus had followed, but it appeared that Dominic had quite other plans.

"Suppose Sister Aloysia, when she finds we aren't in the bus, takes the next bus back to see where we dropped off," he said. "There we should be, her unsuspecting victims, walking innocently along the road. Oh no, we haven't escaped her clutches just for that! We'll find our way back to the river and keep beside it till we get close to the convent; then we'll camp in some very wily place and be off as soon as ever the sun rises tomorrow."

"But do you know at all how far we'd come in the bus before you . . . before you said you began to feel sick?" Josephine asked him.

"Only by the signposts that gave the mileage to Athlone and Carrick—and there were precious few of them that did. But I should say that reckoning between them and the time it took us, it couldn't be much more than about eight miles. And we don't want to arrive at the convent in broad daylight!"

"So we needn't hurry, except to get off this road," said Josephine who, though she had some doubts as to the wisdom of this new journey, could not but feel a lightening of the heart that Ulphin and not Uncle Theo was at the end of it and that it was in their canoe, with a marionette at the prow, and not in a dreary bus in Sister Aloysia's company that they were to travel.

So they stepped out valiantly across some marshy pastures till they reached the river, and then they hastened on for several more miles till by mutual consent they sat down to rest and to make a great hole in one of Sister Philomena's packets of sandwiches. They agreed to keep the other half for an easy supper to eat in the dark, and then there would still be the second packet and the tin of baked beans as provision for their cruise, as well as plenty of money with which to buy food and even ginger pop. Until they were able to go shopping, tea made with boiled river water would have to suffice, and for the present they would have to go thirsty.

"Remember," Josephine adjured her twin who was already casting thirsty glances on the river Shannon, "how nearly you had typhoid fever at Cootehall! Next time it might really be it!" And a dead rat that chose that moment to go cruising past won the battle for her.

Dominic turned out to be an optimist, as Josephine had supposed, and the two children had spent all the afternoon and part of the evening walking upstream before the roofs of Carrick came in sight. It was indeed growing dark, but they kept well out of sight of the convent, for who could tell whether Sister Aloysia had already returned to organize a search party, or whether she had contented herself with a telephone message to Reverend Mother, telling her of their disappearance from the bus?

Fortunately the Yacht Club boat-house was downstream from the convent, so that the stealthy approach near seven o'clock of a pair of footsore and weary twins was observed by none.

In the thickest part of the willows Dominic set up their tent, and in a hollow place she found near by, Josephine lit her fire of dried twigs and brewed the best cup of tea that thirsty children had ever tasted. After that, and with the next morning's early start before them, it was a short step to bed, and very sweet the little noises of the night, the splash of an occasional fish and the wash of ripples against the bank sounded in their ears, nor with such a lullaby as the Shannon sang them was sleep slow in coming that night.

"And to think we might have been back at the Rectory by now!" said Dominic with a sigh of utter contentment.

CHAPTER XI

Where the Lane Led

The sun had not yet risen when Dominic waked Josephine.

"Oh, Dominic," she cried, rubbing eyes still full of sleep. "I was having such a horrid dream. I thought we were back at the Rectory and Uncle Theo had locked us up in the cellar again and told us we couldn't come out till we'd promised never to go out in the canoe again. And Amalthea was bleating for her food and the marionette was crying too, and. . . ."

"It's exactly what will happen," Dominic cut her short, "if you don't get up quickly. I've got out the sandwiches and there's some boiled water over from last night. Oh, *don't* stay to wash!"

"But Sister Philomena told us . . ." Josephine began.

"She'd have told us something different if she'd had Uncle Theo and Sister Aloysia on her track," put in Dominic quickly. "Suppose they come looking for us down the Shannon before we get to Ulphin!"

"Oh, if only we knew how far we have still to go!" Josephine sighed. "But I don't believe they'd really think of looking here first. I daresay Sister Aloysia would tell the Gardai she talked about, and they would scour the country along the bus route first and probably wouldn't notice the canoe had gone till much later."

But she helped Dominic launch the canoe and got in to

eat her sandwiches whilst Dominic paddled away as silently as possible into the twilight; and then when she had done eating, Dominic took his turn with the sandwiches without relinquishing the paddles. Wind and current were there to help them; their hands were growing harder and their arms more accustomed to paddling, and in this way with a good break at midday they covered more miles than on any previous day. At one point, somewhat to their dismay, they seemed to be approaching a town. At a small shop near the river's edge they decided to lay in a store of ginger pop and ask the way to Ulphin. They were served with half a dozen bottles of the drink, but of Ulphin nothing was known.

Unless they had reason for visiting the town, they were advised to take the canal they would presently find on their right, which would shorten their journey considerably and in a mile they would come again to "the very Shannon with four miles or five gained and so much nearer, maybe, to the place ye name, and may God be with you on your way!" said the dear old dame who kept the shop.

They bought some sweets for that and gave her some for herself and all was as she had said till, just before they came back on the very Shannon they came to a lock with a lock-keeper's cottage beyond. Shillings they had and to spare but it was what Dominic called "the publicity" that they dreaded.

"It's the first place they'd ask for news of us, once they'd missed the canoe," Dominic said. "It's really too dangerous. Let's wait here out of sight of the cottage until the light goes, and I believe we could do a carry round."

So they broached the second packet of Sister Philomena's sandwiches, leaving the remainder for breakfast and lunch next day, "and there'll still be the baked beans for supper tomorrow night," said Josephine, "and by that time we'll surely have got to Ulphin, or at least to a shop where we can buy more food."

They emptied the canoe of its cargo to make carrying lighter and then, as daylight faded, by dint of lifting, pulling and pushing, they made the transit successfully and, back on the Shannon, found themselves still so fresh that they decided to push on in the half-dusk, through a little lake to a place where the river seemed to be opening out into a much larger lake. Here, awake to the dangers of lakes, they lit their camp fire and set up their tent. All day long the sun had shone, tempered by a fresh wind that blew them on their way. At no time had they felt so satisfied with their day's progress. Never before had Ulphin seemed so near.

The next day dawned hazy and moist. As Dominic remarked, visibility was bad, but for most of the way across the lough there were buoys to keep them on their course. Then, as the lough showed signs of narrowing, they lost sight of them, which was the more disturbing as several small islands appeared at the same time.

"Let's keep away from islands," Josephine begged. "I shall never like islands again!"

But suddenly, between two islands, a clear way seemed to open and a short distance beyond they passed under a bridge, beside which was a house or two.

"Couldn't we ask the way?" Josephine suggested. "It would be so nice to find someone who knew Ulphin, and we can't be far away now."

But Dominic wouldn't hear of it. "It's just at locks and bridges that everyone asks their questions," he said. " 'Have you seen two children pass this way in a canoe a few hours ago? Two *bad* children?' No, let's go on till we find some nice little quiet cottage tucked away out of sight. Then we'll go and buy some more eggs and, 'Oh, by the way,' I'll say, 'is it much farther to Ulphin?' "

"But if the cottage is out of sight," Josephine began. But by this time they had left the bridge far behind and Dominic was talking about something else.

Again the lough opened out. In another two miles or so out of the mist a second canal suddenly appeared before them. They passed through it to yet another lake. There was no wind today to help them, and even the current seemed dead.

WHERE THE LANE LED

It was past midday and, with the baked beans still to look forward to at supper-time, they ate their remaining sandwiches as they floated on the lake's glassy slate-grey surface. Afterwards, scrupulously tidy in everything concerning their boat, they threw their crumbs overboard and these remained, floating and slowly sinking, exactly where they had thrown them. Again tiny islands appeared, looking overweighted by the heavy trees that grew upon them. The children gave them a wide berth, hugging the lake's western shore, but, as another island loomed out of the haze, they found themselves forced into a deep but narrow channel between it and the shore.

It all happened in a few seconds. There was a violent bump which threw them off their seats, the sound of a crunching tear, and a pointed slimy stake appeared in the bottom of the boat. At the same moment they felt the cold water flowing around their legs, and the canoe slowly filled and sank, leaving them floundering on the surface of the lake. Dominic, with teeth set hard, had made a desperate struggle to paddle the boat closer inshore, but the water already shipped made the effort too much. Though the water was deep they were both good swimmers and not many yards from the shore. In a few strokes they were in their depth and splashing to land. They stood dripping there side by side, their eyes on the place where their boat had disappeared. For a few moments their two bundles remained floating on the surface; then they too, waterlogged at last, slowly sank.

Still dripping and beginning to shiver, the two children turned to each other.

"So what?" asked Dominic.

"So no baked beans for supper," answered Josephine.

For all their different temperaments it seemed that the reactions of these twins when it came to trouble were essentially the same.

It looked like the sort of place where St. George might have killed the dragon. It seemed to be a deep glen, but how high the sides rose no one could tell for they were wrapped in mist. Over its floor a sluggish stream spread, near which a lightly trodden path led away and up where the trees began. Josephine thought it might be nothing but a sheep track, but Dominic pointed out that no sheep, nor traces of them, were visible.

"It's a path that someone must have made some time," he said. "No sheep could have made it so straight."

"Perhaps Some One is dead by now," said Josephine, and fell knee-deep into a hole in the bog.

A mood of hopelessness had fallen upon them; a feeling of oppression that grew as they penetrated deeper into the steep-sided valley round which the mist clung like a miasma. But at least the path was growing clearer and as the valley narrowed to its end they came upon a high but tumble-down stone wall, the fallen stones still lying on the ground as though that strange Some One who seemed about to enter their lives had been too idle or too impotent to pick them up and put them back into place. Together and as though the choice to act was no longer theirs, they clambered over the broken wall and came upon a little one-storeyed cabin with a thatched roof that looked as though the teeth of time had taken many a bite from its edges, and a doorway over which a mass of canariensis tumbled in over-prolific disarray. To Dominic and Josephine the house seemed to belong to some place outside of time.

As they stood hesitating at the doorway there was a sudden scuffle at their feet and a large turkey made a vicious onrush, startling Dominic, who turned to drive it away at the same time that Josephine stepped timidly through the curtain of canariensis to knock on the half-door.

The room, as she gazed inside, looked empty of human habitants, although objects of all kinds were scattered about the floor. There was a spinning-wheel, a broken swift for winding wool, several half-wound skeins hanging on the backs of two chairs, and a fleece dyed blue lying on the floor upon which a large white cat lay luxuriously sleeping.

On the opposite side of the room Josephine could see an alcove hollowed out of the wall, its curtains pulled aside on to blackness. The curtain itself, like the heavy stuff that muffled the window, was made of some dark peacock blue material and had curious designs woven into its fabric of golden stars, crescent moons and concentric circles.

Josephine waited, with Dominic beside her, and the room seemed to wait too to receive them in a silence broken only by the tiny noises of the fire, but she would not heed Dominic's admonition to knock again for she could not escape the conviction which grew with every moment that Some One there already in the shadows was watching them. Then Dominic, leaning past her over the half-door to see what could be seen within started back violently as a voice, soft and quiet, spoke suddenly from somewhere out of sight beside the hearth.

"Come in then, my darlings," it said. "Come in and welcome and take a seat by my fire, for it's cold you are, and hungry maybe and travelled far this day, I can see. Come in and sit down by my side."

Hesitating still, they could not have said why, the two children entered the room. What they saw, seated in the shadows of the hearth, was a pale youngish woman of striking beauty, her ashen-colored hair hanging in two braids beside her face and, between them, two smoke-dark eyes that lingered from one face to the other.

Then they saw that a kettle that hung by a hake over one side of the fire was boiling and that on the other side, balanced on the turf itself, was a girdle covered with steaming potato cakes.

The sight was too much for the children. They decided to accept whatever it might be that the night offered them here and indeed, as the path they had followed had ended at this door, and as the little roof that had hitherto sheltered them was now at the bottom of the lake, there seemed to be no alternative.

Now the woman drew a teapot and some earthenware

mugs out of a cupboard, made tea and handed them each a mug, fetching a jug of milk that stood on the dresser. But Josephine withdrew her mug. "No, we don't drink milk," she cried, faithful always to their vow.

The woman frowned; the smoky eyes glinted. "What is that you say, aroona?" she crooned. "But I think you will drink the milk that I give you. See how creamy is the milk that my goats give!"

"Goats!" cried Josephine and Dominic together. "Do you keep goats? Then, yes please, we'd like some milk very much."

"It's only that cow's milk," Josephine explained, "once made Dominic very ill, and so we made a promise that we'd never drink it again."

The woman muttered, but it was plain that this had made

106

a good impression, and Dominic added, "May we go and see your goats after tea? How many have you got?"

The woman appeared to be counting. "And we know how to milk," added Josephine. "We always milk our own goat, and Nellie, who taught us, says we do it quite well."

"My dears, my darlings," the woman said, and it was evident that nothing could have pleased her better. "Then you shall always milk my goats for me, and help me to make my butter; oh yes, and cheese as well. Would you not like to learn how to make nice cheeses?"

Josephine was sure there was nothing she would like better; Dominic was less certain, but agreed that the butter was very good. Cold and hungry as they were, their tea indeed tasted delicious as they sat eating it on two creepy stools by the fire. The woman, sitting on one of the chairs, continued as she ate to wind unwashed wool from balls into skeins, or washed wool from skeins back into balls again, and in this task she presently asked Josephine to help her and then, as she rose to put tea away, she handed the ball of white wool to Dominic, and watched to see that he wound it in the fashion she approved.

"Why, your clothes is wet," she exclaimed, taking a hand off his shoulder.

"Oh, a little damp," Dominic admitted cautiously. "You see, we fell in the river this morning, but we've been walking all day and they are nearly dry now."

She said nothing to that at first, only eyeing him curiously. "You'll be snug and warm in your beds tonight," she said then, "and by morning your clothes will be dry."

Very odd they felt it to be that she made no effort to learn more about their accident, to call them by their names, or even to ask by what chance they had followed the path that led to her door.

"It suits us," said Dominic in a moment when she had left them alone with the sleeping cat. "Why, she doesn't even seem to take a paper where she might have seen pictures of 'Two Bad Children.' And I don't suppose she sees a Garda from one year's end to another."

"Let's ask her about Ulphin when she comes back," Josephine suggested. "I'm not sure that I like her very much, and I'm quite sure I'd rather be in Ulphin than here in this smothery place."

But when the woman came back it was to tell them to take off their wet clothes at once and go to bed, so that she might begin to get them dry before tomorrow.

"But where are our beds?" Josephine asked, wondering.

"Have you no eyes? There, and there," she replied, pointing to the alcove in the wall which Josephine had noticed on her first arrival, and to another one, curtained like the first, on the opposite side of the room. "And for night clothes you can have these," and she threw them a couple of large brown shawls. "I'll be back for your wet things in a minute."

"But . . ." they both began. But before they had time to finish, she had shut the door upon them.

CHAPTER XII

The Poisoned Glen

Neither Dominic nor Josephine slept much that night. The woman had come back soon afterwards and carried their damp clothing to the fire, after which she had got out her spinning-wheel, removed one shoe, as spinners do, and settled down to spin.

At first the children were fascinated. The wheel, which might have belonged to some long-past age, was painted in bright colors— red, yellow and green. The soft rolls of wool whirled out of the spinner's hand to join the twisting thread, roll after roll disappearing as the bobbin filled, to be wound off into a ball and so back to the beginning again. Better than learning to make cheese, Josephine decided that she would like to become master of this magical thread, which seemed to catch life itself from the spinner's hand. At last the light faded; the woman lit a small oil lamp and set it by her on the table and then, crossing over to the children, pulled each curtain to in front of their alcoves.

"You must lie down and go to sleep now, my dears, my pretties," said she, "and when tomorrow comes, I will let you visit my goats." And she returned to her spinning.

It was dark and rather frightening alone behind those curtains; very much like being shut up in prison, they thought, but the rhythmical whirr of the wheel lulled their senses; their day's wandering had worn them out, and at last they were asleep.

The whirring had ceased and all was quiet and dark in the room when Dominic awoke from a dream of drowning. His head ached, his pulses were throbbing, and inside the alcove it was insufferably hot and airless. He pulled the muffling curtain aside but found the room's atmosphere still unpleasantly close. Flinging out of the shawl's constricting substance, he leapt to the floor and ran naked to the window which at first resisted his efforts to open it but suddenly sprang wide upon a night of a loveliness to which he was no stranger, for he had grown accustomed to sleeping under the sky. Up this one now a full moon was climbing, piercing the trees with its light and illuminating at last the steep sides of the little valley which ended, it seemed, but a short way beyond the cottage. He took several deep breaths, delighting in the fresh sweetness of the night air and then, leaving the window open and his curtain drawn back, slept fitfully for the rest of the night.

Josephine awoke early next morning, her eyes heavy, her head swimming and a feeling of inertia in every limb. For some time she lay as though drugged by the languorous air and then she too, unused to this oppressive darkness, tugged her curtain aside to breathe the fresh morning.

Into the room through the open window the early sun was streaming. It lit on the blue fleece lying on the floor and on the white cat still torpidly sleeping. It lit the gay spinning-wheel, surrounded now by several balls of new wool scattered about the floor, and a stray shaft struck in and picked out Dominic's bare arm dangling over the side of his bunk. Josephine wished that she too had awakened in time to escape the toils of this deadening curtain. Already she felt more like herself, the sense of oppression lifting. She wished that Dominic would wake up, so that they could make some plan together, or perhaps go out to visit the goats.

Then she saw their clothes by the hearth, now completely dry, one set on each side of the fire. It was the work of a moment for her to dress and let herself out by the half-door. The path which had brought them here led on to the back of the house where in a little yard she found the woman of the house busy amongst her goats.

"God's welcome to you, aroona," said she. "I have awaited you this long while and had you delayed much longer I would have broken in on your slumber. There you see is the milking-pail and here my goats. Tethera and Pethera are the large white ones and Hovera and Covera the little browns. Tell me, do you not find them very pretty goats, aroona, say?"

Now to tell the truth and fond as she was of goats, Josephine found them nothing of the kind, but a rather ordinary collection of nannies showing few signs of being either well bred, well fed or even well kept. For all that, it was nice to be back again in the world of goats and, to be quite candid, Josephine was not sorry to have an opportunity to show this strange woman, who seemed to take so little heed of them, that she was no amateur in the art of milking. So she took the milking-pail and the stool that was handed to her and had just settled down to milk Covera, the smallest of the goats, when Dominic appeared round the corner of the cottage.

"How late you are, my darling," the woman greeted him. "I think you must have slept too well in my soft bed. It is no lazy basking boy, I would have you to know, that stays on in my cottage. Go you now and pick some outside leaves off yon cabbage plants and put them in that little house for my goats."

Dominic, who had bridled at this mode of address, went off without a word to the row of cabbages but paused before throwing the leaves into the house.

"Perhaps you don't know it," he said then, as politely as might be, "but this house is not very clean."

"How true that is, my love, my darling," the woman answered, and her voice was as soft as a caress. "And you, I can see, are one that will always attend to the wants of the poor dumb animals before your own. Now take that shovel in the corner there by the door. It will be nothing to you,

surely, a fine great boy like yourself, to have the house fresh
and nice and worthy of my beautiful goats, the poor crea-
tures! And your sister and I will be going within and keeping
the porridge hot for your breakfast, so make no delay."

And, taking the milking-pail from Josephine, who had
found the little goat Covera nearly dry, she led the way into
the house, leaving Dominic setting to work with a broken-
down shovel to clear away two solid feet of rotted food and
dung.

As they entered the room where the children had passed
the night the woman gave a cry of dismay. "Who has opened
my window?" she exclaimed, "letting all the cold air of the
night into the room. Look you, even my poor cat has left me,
he who dreams here always by the fire."

The cat's place was indeed empty, nothing but his shape
still impressed upon the blue fleece to show where he had
lain. "Did you do this?" asked the woman, slamming the
window to with a rattle of panes.

Josephine shook her head. "I don't know who did it," she
truthfully said, "but the room was very stuffy when we went
to sleep."

The woman croaked. "Those who don't like a warm bed
had best stay outside in the rain," she said. "Two tramping
children!" she added as though to herself. But even as she
spoke she set a plateful of steaming porridge in front of
Josephine, who felt at once that this was no moment to pick
a quarrel which, indeed, Dominic was only too likely to do
before many hours were past.

Thinking of this possibility with dismay, she decided to
take the first opportunity to confer with her twin as to the
future which, except for a few coins in Dominic's pocket,
seemed to consist of nothing but liabilities.

With the idea of healing any possible breach, she began
tactfully to engage the woman in a conversation about spinning, and by the time Dominic entered the room, had ex-
tracted from her a promise which seemed to be given with
surprising willingness that before the day was over she would

begin to teach her to spin. Dominic, to her relief, sat down too hungry for anything but silence, and when he did begin to talk, his mood seemed one of unexpected mildness.

"Those are very pretty nannies that you have there," he began, avoiding as he spoke his sister's eyes, which were looking at him in some amazement. "You can see from their sleek wedge-shaped bodies that they have plenty of breeding in them."

The woman put an extra spoonful of porridge on to his plate. "It is true," she said, "that they have every point that a good goat should have. Only the coat is perhaps a little short for spinning, but I hope to mend that before long."

"Indeed," Dominic said. "And I'm sure, as you seem to have no billy-goat of your own, that you must have some very fine ones in this neighborhood?"

Now Josephine perceived where the conversation was leading.

"My cousin," said the woman, "has an old billy-goat that is the father of the two white nannies, but he's nothing but a poor old puck with no ancestry in him at all, as I'm always for telling him. There's no goat about here fit to mate with my pretty nannies."

Dominic said nothing, but it was clear to Josephine that he was greatly disappointed.

There were more potato cakes for breakfast, but they had been nicer when they were newly made. When breakfast was finished and cleared away, the woman gave Dominic two buckets and sent them to fill him at the stream. "Now girl," she said then, seating herself in one of the chairs and pointing to a creepy stool, "you are after asking me to teach you the way to spin and I will now begin to show you. But first, get me that bundle of wool you see wrapped in paper on the shelf. 'Tis a little soiled it is, but 'twill serve well enough and you who are learning would destroy good fleece by your mistakes. And bring me my carders, those boards fitted with spikes you see on the shelf below, for you must first learn how wool should be carded."

Obediently Josephine fetched the objects indicated and

laid them on the woman's lap. The scrap of fleece was certainly very dirty and reeked of sheep, but Josephine was always one to take the rough with the smooth where animals were concerned. The carders were two bits of wood of rather the shape and size of a hand mirror, except that they had squared instead of rounded sides. But instead of mercury and glass, their faces bristled with stiff little wires, about three-quarters of an inch in depth, which were to act as a comb for combing out the knots and tails in the wool.

Now began a process which at first Josephine felt she would never be clever enough to learn but when, after nearly a morning's work, she was able to turn the tangled fleece into soft little rolls ready for spinning, the woman left her and went out to join Dominic who was now sawing logs outside the kitchen door.

Josephine was glad to be quit of that over-soft voice, of those cold damp hands that had guided hers throughout the lesson, and she envied Dominic his work outside by the stream and in the wood where he had been sent to collect fallen branches. But presently, hearing loud sounds of altercation outside the back door, she hurried out to find him and his instructress at opposite ends of a two-handed saw, calling each other by other names than "my darling". The woman had a bleeding hand for which she was crying out that Dominic was to blame, whilst he, looking mulish, had succeeded in getting the saw so firmly wedged in the damp wood that it could not be moved in either direction.

"Give me the girl!" she cried angrily, catching sight of Josephine in the doorway. "The girl for me, and never this great stupid omadaun of a boy! Look you," she went on, "this pile of wood has to be sawn before dinner can be cooked. If not, no wood to cook with, no dinner. You have only to choose!"

Dominic, his face very red, tugged out the saw at last and laid it down. "I think," he said, and his voice was shaking, "if you take the other handle off and let me use the saw alone, I shall get your wood sawn in far less time."

"By the holy angels, take it then!" the woman cried angrily and pitched the saw across to him, narrowly missing Josephine where she stood by the door. "Let you get on with the sawing alone. I'll not ease your work; come girl!" and she flung into the house just in time to miss "You certainly won't!" as Dominic got in the last word.

"Don't let her teach you how to card!" Josephine whispered to him as she followed her taskmaster into the house.

"What! Have you been playing cards?" Dominic's voice followed her incredulously. But there was no time to tell him how great was his mistake.

"Now my darling, my good little girl." Josephine writhed as she awaited the next inspiration on the part of her ingenious tormentor. It seemed like a game of forfeits in which she was always the loser. "Come with me and we will churn the cream together to make the butter from the milk of my goats. And when that is done, you and your brother can take them out into the glen and see that they do not pull up their tethering pegs and stray away, for it's hungry they are and wild and not easily satisfied with what is given them."

When the cream was churned, the flecks of butter showing in the glass window of the churn, Josephine and Dominic went gladly with the four goats to the glen, but the pasture was poor and what there was the goats only nibbled at and then stood looking at their keepers and bleating as though they were children complaining that they do not care for fish for dinner.

"And yet they're so gaunt and thin," Josephine said, stroking the little brown nanny that she had milked. "And you know, Covera, you hardly gave any milk this morning!"

"Let's take them up to the other side of the valley," Dominic suggested. "Perhaps they don't care about the grass in this stuffy place. And I wonder what is this queer sort of weed that grows everywhere?" He plucked a plant and held it out to the other brown nanny, which barely sniffed it and tugged again at her tether.

So children and goats climbed to the farther side of the

valley and here, indeed, the goats settled down to graze and before very long were chewing the cud as though at last they had found a breakfast to their satisfaction.

When evening's milking-time came round, with Dominic and Josephine in charge of a milking-pail apiece, the goats were found to have given a far greater quantity of milk than usual.

"Why, my darlings, my good little children," the woman exclaimed. "It's you shall milk my goats each day, morning and evening, for your reward; yes, and take them out to pasture too till milking-time comes round again."

"I shall like that far better than carding," Josephine told Dominic as soon as they were out of earshot, "and it's a change, anyway, to be called good!"

" 'Good little children'—ugh!" Dominic exclaimed. "I'd rather be Sister Aloysia's Bad Children—if it wasn't for the goats. I believe she starves them in that valley!"

CHAPTER XIII

At Last!

And so a week passed, or it might have been ten days, for the children soon lost count of time in a world where all days, week-days and Sundays, were exactly alike, and each of them, in this atmosphere of languorous boredom, twice as long as in the free world outside.

"You'd think we were her slaves!" Dominic cried one day when he had gone as usual to fill the buckets at the stream and met Josephine who, armed with a whip, had been sent to watch the young turkeys, which had taken to straying of late.

"I shouldn't mind so much doing all these dull things," said Josephine, "if I liked her even a little. But I haven't ever hated anybody so much. Do you think she's a witch?"

"I shouldn't be surprised at anything," answered Dominic. "Can't you almost feel her trying to put a spell on us so that we shall never go away?"

"She certainly doesn't want us to go," Josephine remarked.

"And can you wonder?" cried Dominic. "We hew her wood and draw her water; we milk her goats and make her butter and her cheese. . . ."

"Yes, and I have to card her horrible dirty wool," added Josephine, "and I don't believe she ever means to teach me to spin, which is the one thing I should like to do. And now I've got the turkeys to look after as well!" She cracked the turkeys' whip viciously and they ran gobbling away as fast as their pigwidgeon legs would carry them. "I can't imagine what she'd do if we left her!"

"*If* we left her!" cried Dominic. "There's no if in it. You know we've only waited to give the hue and cry a chance to die down, and the weather to clear up, and to find out where we are and where the river Shannon is, and we'd be off to Ulphin in no time!"

"Do you think we'd lost the river Shannon again then?" Josephine inquired anxiously.

"I wasn't sure. All that last day I'd had my doubts. I don't believe the Shannon flows through such a number of small lakes. And then do you remember the way the current had died away? I didn't say anything because it would have made us too miserable to think we'd gone wrong again, but I was feeling pretty depressed already when we ran on to that stake."

"If only we could find someone who could tell us the way to Ulphin!" Josephine wailed. "Oh well . . . I wonder why she wanted us to be so quick this morning?"

"Some other ghastly duty waiting for us, I suppose. Let's be as slow as we possibly can," Dominic suggested.

So it was a good hour later when they returned at snail's pace to the house. But for once the woman seemed in too much of a stir to have any sarcastic comment to make. "How dirty you look!" was all she said. "It's time you had another bath in the lake! But not now. Go and get your mackintoshes on quickly. We are taking Hovera and Covera for a walk."

"Now, in the rain?" exclaimed Dominic. "Won't it do after we've had our dinner?"

"It will not. And it will be a long walk, I'm telling you, and we're taking our dinner with us to eat by the way. 'Tis yourself will carry it," she finished, thrusting a package into Dominic's hands. "I have the goats on their leashes and you can lead one each. They know you and will lead easily, and when we come to the road, there'll likely be a boy with a pony cart waiting for us."

The children brightened at this. It reminded them of ex-

peditions with Jim Lyons in those days at the Rectory, a
life which after all, they sometimes allowed, had quite a few
compensations which the present one lacked.

After about half an hour's walking along a trackway which
led to some flattish country where at any moment a river
might have appeared, they came upon a small walled country lane with a cottage or two upon it and a pony and four-
wheeled market cart in which sat a big hulking boy of about
fifteen.

The woman greeted him as Jamesey, and explained that he
was her cousin's child, but though it was their arrival that
he was apparently awaiting, the boy made no attempt to
leave his seat and help her and the two children to load the
goats on to the cart. He held the reins and surveyed the party
with an eye in which interest quickly flagged, whilst the two
children heaved up Hovera and Covera and fastened the
sheep net over the cart. Then they mounted and sat beside
the other two on the seat that ran the width of the cart, and
the cavalcade set off at a brisk trot along the road which led
towards the distant hills.

Dominic and Josephine exchanged glances and smiled.
Any change seemed welcome in their present circumstances
and, once quit of the enervating airs of the closed-in valley,
their spirits rapidly rose. It was a wide empty country that
they were travelling through; the clouds had passed over the
land already to darken the eastern hills, only their shadows
lingering, following them over those hills like sheep their
shepherd. Everything here gave fair promise for the future,
and a cool wind blew freshly in their faces. Even the torpid
boy began to whistle and, encouraged by such a phenomenon,
Dominic sought to engage him in conversation.

"By the look of the sun," he began, "we must be going
about due south."

The boy turned heavy eyes towards the sun. "Oh ay?" he
answered tonelessly, "is that so?"

"And the river Shannon, would that be to the east or the
west of us?" Dominic pursued.

"Maybe I could tell ye if I knew which was one and which the other," the boy replied.

"If we're going south, the east is on our left and the west on our right," Dominic prompted him.

"The river Shannon is at the back of me head," the boy answered with finality. "And phwat are ye gettin' at with all your questions at all?" And a sulky look came over his face.

"Och, don't be answering him now," his cousin put in quickly. "He's up to no good with all his geography."

"Only tell me one more thing," Dominic begged. "That tall peak in front of us, what mountain is that?"

" 'Tis the White Mountain, and me coosin says I'm to tell ye no more," and the boy subsided into a lethargic silence, even his whistling ended.

After some time they came to a cross-road and then, about two miles farther on, a smithy. Here they all got down. For the boy and pony cart this was the end of their outward journey, for the pony was to have four new shoes, whilst the others continued their journey on foot.

The children, leading the goats, followed the woman to a mounting lane which grew slightly steeper and then petered out. But a footpath led on up beside a streamlet that leapt to meet them. This was a country made for goats and children, and they bounded upwards together by large stones that seemed fitted to their feet, exulting in the freedom of movement and, whether children or goats, in the company of each other. But the woman, all her breath needed for the steep ascent, her tongue quelled, her powers gone, was making heavy going of this journey, wherever it might lead. Alternately cursing the steepness of the climb and the slippery stones beside the stream, the goats that set the pace and the children that followed, she presented a spectacle that even Dominic took pity on, and he endeavored to curb his goat Hovera's eager progress.

"And Covera's just as bad," cried Josephine, both hands on the little goat's tether and leaning back in a vain effort

to slacken the pace. "You'd think she knew where she was going; I only wish we did!"

Beneath them the country through which they had driven stretched out; the smithy, the cross-roads and even a long blue river—could it be the very Shannon, winding from the far side of this mountain that they were climbing. But above their heads nothing but shelf after shelf of hillock and hollow.

Now the path seemed to be leading into a high green valley between the mountain's two heads, where the waters of the stream had collected into a tiny lake. The sun, so long hidden by the mountain's northerly slope, was shining gaily and the cold wind gone.

"Oh," cried Josephine on a long breath. "Look at the foxgloves, there, beside that blue lake! And look, aren't there water-lilies on it too?"

"I was really looking for goats," Dominic told her. "Can't you smell them? It can't be our two nannies. There must be a whole herd of them somewhere quite near!"

As he spoke there reached them over the hill the small drone of the Irish pipes and turning quickly in the direction

of the sound, they saw a herd of black goats descending the path.

Dominic and Josephine looked at each other, their breath held, their eyes bright with an incredulous question. There was no need for any spoken word. Then they looked back at the goats as they came gambolling down the mountain-side.

"It's the very tune that Miley sang," cried Dominic. "I've remembered it at last!"

"But where is he, the Green-coated Boy?" Josephine asked, her voice hushed with awe.

"There, just behind," cried Dominic, "but you can't see him because he's the same color as the hill."

CHAPTER XIV

The Green-coated Boy

The Green-coated Boy was sitting with Dominic and Josephine beside the stream, his goats behind him nibbling the grass of the mountain. The woman had gone on in the direction of a cottage that appeared in the hollow, saying that she wished nothing so much as to rest her feet.

"You can let your goats go free," the boy told the children. "Now they are here they will find no better pasture, nor company either."

The children unfastened the leads and in a moment Hovera and Covera had capered off to join the herd.

" 'Twas one of our billies that fathered those two," the Boy remarked, "but 'twas from a pair of white goats as ugly as any you'd see that they were bred. It's nice little goats they are growing for all that, now they have a little more food in their bellies. Is it you that is keeping the goats for Herself?"

"Not longer than we can help!" Dominic answered. "We don't really belong to her at all. We don't even know her name, nor she ours."

"You see," Josephine explained, "we had a shipwreck on the river, and so wandered about all day in the hills trying to find somewhere to shelter in and towards evening we came to her cottage and—we've been there ever since."

· "God and Mary save us," said the Boy, "that would be a

terrible thing to happen to anybody. And what were you doing coming down the river in a boat?"

"We were looking for you!" Dominic threw himself backwards on the grass, laughing hugely. It all seemed such an excellent joke now that they were sitting here beside him.

"Sure, ye're mad!" said the Boy, smiling good-naturedly. "Come on and tell me truly."

"You see, we have a very beautiful little goat," said Josephine, beginning at one end of the story.

"But you don't know anything about her," Dominic took up the tale in another place. "But there's a man called Miley. He's lame and he plays the fiddle."

"And I can't say I know anything about *him*," said the Boy, looking with growing bewilderment from one to the other.

"But Miley knows a drover whose name is Black Michael," Dominic continued, watching the Boy closely.

"Ah, now we're coming to it!" cried he. "And come to think of it, there is a lame fiddler comes here sometimes in the company of that one, and maybe his name will be Miley as likely as any other, for I've never heard it at all."

"And Miley," Dominic continued, "told me that our goat, Josephine's and mine, was one of the most beautiful little nannies he'd seen anywhere, except at Ulphin, and he said the only goats that could compare with her were the ones bred here on the mountain that was 'down the river and over the hill.' You had one, he said, that was a veritable Prince of Pucks!"

"Tell me now," said the Green-coated Boy, his face alight with excitement, "is it a little white nanny-goat is yours that Miley saw? Indeed then, he told us of that very one, even to her name; Agatha I think was the name he called her by."

"Not Agatha, but Amalthea," Dominic interposed, "and Uncle Theo, who's very clever as well as rather silly, says that the first goat Amalthea was the foster-mother of a god."

"Do you tell me so?" exclaimed the Green-coated Boy, greatly impressed.

"And we thought," put in Josephine, "that if we could buy or borrow one of your Prince of Puck's sons, then we might have a regular royal family of goats of our own."

"So that's the long and the short of it," said the Boy, his eyes like two green wells of laugher. "And you to come all the way down the Shannon to find us, the Prince of Pucks and me! Look ye now," he became meditative; "I will take ye to my grandfer, for 'tis he must settle this thing. But I'll tell ye this; he was listening with me to Miley's talk of a little white goat up in the north called Agatha that would make his own herd look like a lot of runts, and it was black looks of envy that my granfer was giving him. But the old man said to me afterwards, 'If I could have a kid from this Agatha now, white or black, would it not be a grand herd we should be building up on this mountain? In the whole of Ireland there would be no herd the like of ours!' But come now with me and we will go find my granfer, and sure, when he hears 'tis yourselves that has the little white goat, he will be mad with wanting to steal her away from you, and it's no lie I am telling you!"

So the three of them set off down the path that led, just as Miley had described it, to a little stone cabin on the farther side of the stream, which they crossed by stepping-stones, and everywhere the proud heads of the foxgloves were nodding. But from inside the cottage they heard voices raised in loud altercation.

"Hearken to me, woman; it's no goat of mine ye'll have to feed or starve on your poisonous pasture. It's shamed I'd be to have my pucks father any creature that's to bide in such a place, to fare in such a way! Take your nannies back the way they came, and let's hear no more about it, now nor at any future time."

Dominic and Josephine hung back, feeling that this was no time for an introduction so momentous, and they heard the soft voice answer in blandishing tones, "But man, dear, what am I but a poor weak woman with a delicate chest, not fit at all to take such a great climbing journey. . . ."

THE GREEN-COATED BOY

At this point the Green-coated Boy pushed his way past and entered the room, the children following behind in some trepidation at breaking in upon such a scene.

"Don't heed her, Granfer," said the Boy. "Hearken to what these two have to say. Tell out, now, what you're after telling me, of your little white goat Agatha that the lame fiddler was for making such a frish-frash about not long since. Faith, Granfer, 'tis for that same goat that these two have come to see ye today, and they travelling the country in a boat and sinking to the bottom of the Shannon for nothing but to find her a mate here that would be worthy of her!"

Dominic and Josephine were able at last to give their attention to the little old man who now turned upon them a pair of bright and very dark eyes that a moment since had been darting glances of fire at the woman, their companion.

"In the name of God," he said, "if it's the truth ye are telling, ye may take your pick of any of the pucks that ye see here, and not a pennypiece will I ask of ye, only that when that one has had two kids, whether at one birth or two, ye will give the one of them to me, whenever I ask ye for it."

His eyes on them, his lively face expressing eager inquiry, he waited for them to speak. But the twins, finding themselves confronted almost too suddenly with the answer to all their dreams, still hesitated.

"Of course you could have a kid," said Dominic at last, "and we'd be as proud as proud to have one of your billies . . ." He paused.

"So that's settled then," said the old goatherd, "and the Boy here will take ye to the mountain to make your choice, and we'll find ye a lead for getting him home." He looked at them closely and said a few words in Irish to the Boy, and they all went out together, leaving the woman who, having settled herself on a low chair by the turf fire, said she would rest her feet for half an hour before making the descent.

The Boy, followed by Dominic and Josephine, took a path that led up one side of the hill. "It's no liking me granfer has for that one," the Boy remarked as soon as they were out of earshot of the cottage. " 'Tis only the half of her is of our people, and the other half nothing but a tinker, God help her, with no understanding of the animals, nor of how they should be rightly kept. And the pastures in her glen is all poisoned with spurge; no animal will thrive there, no, nor childer either. It's yourselves should begone before worse befalls ye, for I can see ye've but little flesh on ye already and less still ye'll have the longer ye stay."

"It's not that we like being with her," Dominic explained, "but we had a sort of idea that with nannies of her own, she might know the way to this place, and it seems we weren't far wrong! Now, if you think your grandfather's going to give us one of his billies to take back to Amalthea, we shall escape as soon as we can. But we're ever so far from home, and our boat is sunk, even if we could ever have persuaded your billy to travel in it, and. . . ."

"I have it!" said the Green-coated Boy. "In the week that's coming, Black Michael, the drover, will be taking his cattle truck with a bull in it to a gentleman at Castle Fogarty. Let you be about on the Lanesborough road—will ye mind that? —and he will take yourselves and the puck as far as Holy Cross, and there ye will find some of our own people, travellers but not tinkers, with their van, who will be starting northwards in one week's time or two, as their way is at this season. If ye'll tell them 'twas the Green-coated Boy that asked it, they will take ye, sure, to any place ye name."

"And how shall we know them when we get there?" asked Dominic, his face already eager for the meeting.

"Faith, there's no other van but theirs travels the road between Holy Cross and Cashel of the Kings. It's great musicians they are, every one of them, with their harp and their fiddle and their pipes. It is from themselves I had these very ones—my grandfer has it there's not a family of finer musicians in the land, but it's blind they are from birth, my sorrow 'tis to tell ye so!"

"Did you say there's one that plays the harp, and is she

Kathleen Hogan?" Josephine exclaimed. "Sister Philomena at the convent told us about her," she continued. "She even remembered a little bit of your song that she sang there; the same song that Miley had sung to Dominic."

"Indeed, she's the very same," cried the Green-coated Boy. "And which of my songs was that one, for it's many I've sung in this place or that place, walking the green hills of Ireland?"

"Oh, it was a song about . . ." Josephine looked across to Dominic for prompting, for she was one of those to whom it is penance to learn poetry by heart.

"It went like this," and, forgetting to be self-conscious, Dominic sang,

> *A land of beauty, a land of truth*
> *Where youth shall never grow old, or pine.*

You were playing the tune on your pipes as we came along the path," he added.

"Yes, and there was some more about hair of primrose hue and a cheek glowing like a foxglove," put in Josephine eagerly. "That was the song the blind harpist sang to Sister Philomena in the women's ward. . . ."

"And all the old ladies stopped quarrelling and became quite docile," added Dominic. "I say, Josephine, I wonder what would happen if he sang it to our witch!"

The Boy shook his head laughing. "I will not sing that song to the like of herself," he said.

"But is it really true," Dominic asked, "that nothing here —not you, nor your goats nor even the foxgloves will ever grow old or die? Not ever?" he repeated.

"Faith, no!" the Green-coated Boy answered more seriously. "We're all but mortal like any others. 'Tis not here is that land at all. The land of which the song tells is Tir nan Og, the Land of Youth. It is the land to which our people fled, some say, when they were driven out of Ireland by the invaders who came next. They tell it to be a fair island in the stream of the western ocean. Some say it van-

ished out of sight long since, and others that there are islands
where our people still live on, but it's the way it is, the
islands are not always to be seen; but whether it is that they
have the power to sink beneath the waves, or to make themselves invisible to the men of today, I cannot rightly say. But
this I will tell you; that song was sung by a prince of that
race when he came back to fetch his lady-love away from the
enemy king who was for claiming her as well as the kingdom
of Ireland."

"And did she go?" asked Josephine.

"There's never been any yet," the Boy asserted, "that
doesn't follow after where that song and its singer leads."

"Won't you sing it to us?" Josephine pleaded. "Only I
suppose it's written in Irish and we shan't understand it."

"So it was. But there was a great Irish scholar who was a
poet himself, and he set it all over again to English words.
Yes, I'll sing it to you, sure, but you'll remember that the
next time you hear that song, it may be yourselves as well as
the goats that has to up and follow after!"

They willingly agreed, and the Green-coated Boy without
more ado and with his eyes on the goats who slowly gathered
round, sang Midir's Call to Fairy Land.

> *Come back to me, lady, to love and to shine*
> *In the land that was thine in the long-ago,*
> *Where of primrose hue is the golden hair*
> *And the limbs are fair as the wreathèd snow.*
>
> *To the lakes of delight that no storm may curl*
> *Where the teeth are as pearl, the eyes as sloes,*
> *Which alight, whenever they choose to seek,*
> *On the bloom of a cheek, where the foxglove glows.*
>
> *Each brake is alive with the flowers of spring,*
> *Whence the merlins sing in their shy retreat;*
> *Though sweet be the meadows of Innisfail,*
> *Our beautiful vale is far more sweet.*

THE GREEN-COATED BOY

Though pleasant the mead be of Innisfail,
  More pleasant the ale of that land of mine,
A land of beauty, a land of truth,
  Where youth shall never grow old, or pine.

From thence we see, though we be not seen,
  We know what has been and shall be again,
And the cloud that was raised by the first man's fall
  Has concealed us all from the eyes of men.

Then come with me, lady, to joys untold,
  And a circlet of gold on thy head shall be,
Banquets of milk and of wine most rare,
  Thou shalt share, O lady, and share with me.[1]

They had followed the Boy to a place where the young goats were feeding, one of their number mounted on a rock playing sentry to the others.

"Isn't he marvellous!" Josephine cried, pointing at this young billy where he stood outlined against the skyline, the shaggy black head and graceful horns a challenge to all that came.

"Ay, it's a good one enough is that one," the Boy allowed, "and you may be sure the others are of the same mind or he wouldn't be up there now. Give him another two months or so to grow strength into his horns, and he'll be a match for any old puck in the herd."

"Oh, please," Josephine begged, "couldn't he be the one we choose for ourselves? Of course they're all beautiful, but this one is something more than beautiful. I'm certain he's clever and brave as well."

The Green-coated Boy laughed his approval. " 'Tis you is the goat fancier, I do believe!" he said, "and it's me granfer will be pleased 'tis the one you've picked. Come then,

[1] From *The Wooing of Etain,* a very ancient poem of Pagan Ireland, translated by Dr. Douglas Hyde. It is the subject of Rutland Boughton's beautiful and far too rarely heard opera, *The Immortal Hour.*

Yanadick, let you follow your new master and mistress from now on and do their bidding, and maybe there will be a fairy princess at the end of your journey!"

He approached the goat quietly, motioning the children to stay where they were, and although the rest of the herd scattered, the young sentry goat stood his ground and allowed the Boy to pass the end of the cord round his neck.

The children came up to look him in the face and coax his long black coat and the young goat, fearless still, looked back at them with a gaze that was at once benevolent and debonair. They were delighted, and when the Boy put the other end of the lead into Josephine's hand, she felt it to be the proudest moment of her life.

The Boy looked at the sky. "The shadows are lengthening," he said. " 'Tis time, I'm thinking that th'auld witch was on her homeward journey; but mind, no pasturing for this one in the Poisoned Glen or ye'll maybe never take him out of it again."

Now Dominic thought of something else. "How shall we know which day to go walking on the Lanesborough road?" he asked. "We can't just go there next Monday morning and wait there till Saturday! And will it be the road that crossed the one we came here by?"

"Ay, the very same," the Boy assured him. "And as for Black Michael, he will be coming up here at the same time with a keg of poteen for my granfer, and I will get word to you by some means the day he's travelling the road. And mind you that herself keeps her hands off of our puck, or ye'll ask in vain for me granfer to give ye another."

They promised and, with Yanadick following easily by the lead in Josephine's hand, they returned to the cottage and were joined by the old goatherd who was carrying a sackful of turf down the hill.

"It is even the one I should have chosen myself," he said with an approving glance at Josephine and Yanadick. "A Prince of Pucks is he, and sure will do honor to your herd, and his young kid a great ornament to mine the day it comes.

A nanny or a puck, a black or a white, it's all one to me. But mind," he continued, shaking a threatening finger as he saw the woman emerge from his house, "it's to yourselves I am giving him, and to no other, and the sooner you take him away from the Glen, the better 'twill be for all of you." And he made a menacing gesture in her direction.

"There now," said the woman as she came smiling up to them, her eyes feasting on Yanadick. "I made sure you'd let me have one of your billies when all the talking was done. And it's a fair price I'll pay ye for this one, for it's good blood he has, I can see it well, and 'tis he will raise me a herd will make my cousin sick for envy."

"Put your purse by, woman!" said the old goatherd. "It isn't money I'd take for that one. 'Tis to these children I have given him, so make an end of your talk for it's never another one of mine will feed in your glen."

"Indeed, it's a wonderful present you have made to my darlings," she said. "It's good and obedient children they are as you can see, well deserving the nice home I have made for them in the glen. But come now, girleen dear, fetch the two nannies back from the hill, for it's time we were away now, and Jamesey waiting us there below."

CHAPTER XV

On the Road Again

So with Yanadick on his lead they returned to the glen and on the surface life resumed its round of disagreeable duties, but on the surface only. Sometimes the woman wondered at the children's improved spirits, their listlessness gone, their eyes bright again with something that had no apparent cause, unless it might be the delight they took in the new billy-goat. Indeed she took a great pleasure and pride in Yanadick herself as she watched him playfully gambolling with the children in his young might and grace. She had even invited her old cousin to come one day and look at her new billy, well knowing that the old man's heart would be scalded with covetousness at the sight. She was expecting him that very morning, and was already listening for the sound of his pony's hooves on the track through the glen when it occurred to her that the children were late coming in for their dinner, and they knowing all about the potato cakes she had ready fizzling on the girdle, for had they not themselves peeled the potatoes, singing some sort of a queer song as they did so?

She paused in the middle of turning the cakes at the sound of a far-away something to which she had listened before, either that morning or at some other time, without much heeding it. Almost a tune it seemed, or was it a humming on one note only, as of a flight of swarming bees? She stepped outside to listen, but now what she heard was the sound of her cousin's pony cart jolting up the glen. Hugging herself in anticipation as she thought of the contrast between Yanadick and her cousin's old billy, she returned to continue the turning of the cakes on the girdle.

Dominic and Josephine were talking again of Ulphin; of what they had imagined, and of the reality. Their thoughts were still in some confusion, Dominic disappointed that the Land of Youth of Miley's song was still to seek, buried at the bottom of the sea or swallowed in the mists of the western ocean; whilst Josephine was completely contented with the Ulphin that they had found, with the Green-coated Boy and his promise to set them free, and of his almost miraculous present of Yanadick, the Prince of Pucks of their dreams, whom she already adored.

"I wonder when we shall see the Green-coated Boy again," mused Dominic. "He said he'd send word to us when Black Michael was on his way, or do you think he may perhaps come himself to tell us?"

"That would be best of all," meditated Josephine, "but he seems to have such a horror of this place—the Poisoned Glen as he calls it, that I can't imagine. . . ."

"Then listen to that!" said Dominic. He held up his hand and his eyes were shining in the way Josephine knew so well. And there they were, the pipes of the Green-coated Boy, but playing from so very far away that they had to strain their ears to make sure they were not mistaken.

But someone else had heard them too. Yanadick, who had been grazing nearby, was moving off slowly, his ears cocked in the direction from which the pipes were sounding, his long tether and the pin that had held it dragging together across the turfy grass. He was mounting to the top of the hill bounding the valley on its southern side, and would very soon have vanished from sight over the top.

"Yanadick!" Josephine called, for she had seen to it that the goat knew his name. "Yanadick, come back!"

"Yanadick," her twin echoed her, "wait for us!" And the

two children pelted up the hill just in time to see the goat break into a run at the top. It was a good race, for pursuers and pursued were equally matched, but the goat maintained his lead, leaping the tussocks nimbly where the children stumbled through them, dancing the lighter while their footsteps dragged until they were near despair. As if to discourage them further the music they had heard had by now completely died away and, as there had never been sign of any musician, it was only too easy to believe that what they had taken to be the Green-coated Boy's call belonged to the realm of fancy and that in a very short time Yanadick would have vanished into it as well. Josephine could have wept at the tragedy of it all had she not felt that she needed every scrap of breath to run with. And far indeed it seemed to them that they had followed behind a goat who was no longer even in sight when they came at length upon a distant view of the road that they had crossed in the pony cart on their way to the smithy—the Lanesborough road.

At this point, as good luck would have it, Yanadick in descending to the road had got his lead caught up in the broken branch of a tree. There he stood, at the end of his tether indeed, his head bowed down, his whole attitude submissive as the children bent to unloose his cord.

"So now, what?" asked Josephine, feeling that any proposal that they should return to their former bondage should never come from her. The question seemed to take the last breath left in her body so that when Dominic suggested that the three of them should now sit by the roadside and rest themselves, she felt a rush of gratitude.

So they sat on and after a while, as breath returned, Josephine began a long dialogue with the goat, upbraiding him tenderly for his lack of feeling in leaving his rightful owners at the call of one who had no more claim on him, and an imaginary call at that. And the goat responded by sniffing the air in this quarter and that, and alternately cocking his ears in the direction in which the alluring sounds had ceased and waggling them backwards the better to hear the tones of her voice. Dominic listened to this conversation indulgently till suddenly, he jerked himself into attention and told his sister rather abruptly to "Shut up!"

"Don't you hear anything?" he asked as she turned to him for an explanation.

"What is it?" Josephine cried, hearing something indeed but not quite certain what it might be, and then they both jumped to their feet, for what they saw was a large cattle truck which as it approached nearer, turned out to be driven by a gigantic man who might have been a descendant of one of the crew of the Spanish Armada, so blue-black was his hair, so aquiline his broken nose.

"It must be Black Michael, and I expect he's been sent here by the Green-coated Boy," cried Dominic in a state of high excitement, and he leapt into the road and began waving the painted mackintosh, which he had taken off during the chase, in the direction of the approaching truck.

The man driving it was for swerving to avoid him, but at that moment Josephine with Yanadick in tow joined Dominic on the road and immediately the truck pulled to a halt.

As it did so, from the inside of the truck came a terrific bellow, and the white face and reddish eyes of an enormous Hereford bull appeared between two timbers of the truck. Josephine hastily drew back and even Yanadick seemed a little shaken. Only Dominic's faith in the Green-coated Boy gave him courage as he climbed on to the step of the truck and asked in a firm voice, "Are you Black Michael?"

"I am he," replied the big man in a bass rumble of a voice, "and is it yourselves are the travelling children with the Ulphin puck? Indeed then, ye're to come with me, for the Boy has asked it himself, and if ye'll bide a minute, I'll fix it so ye can have a place in here behind the Castle Fogarty bull, and himself not able to get at ye at all."

Josephine and the goat were still inclined to hang back, and even when Black Michael had rearranged the compartment so that the bull could do no more than glower at them, they seemed to have no great enthusiasm for the ride.

"Come on, up you go!" Dominic prompted them, and without more ado picked up Yanadick in his arms and hoisted him into the truck. Only then did Josephine overcome her native distrust of all things bovine and climb in beside her two companions.

Black Michael looked over his shoulder, nodded to them and started the truck, and then began a lengthy journey that would have been most tedious had it not been for the extremely pointed way in which the bull showed his dislike of the new arrangement. It was not so much against the children that he demonstrated his antagonism as against Yanadick, at whom he glowered and bellowed in turn whilst the young goat, offended at first, was soon in a state of abject terror from which Dominic only saved him by using the painted mackintosh as a curtain and hanging it between their goat and those awesome bloodshot eyes.

So the hours passed and the miles too, though little of the country through which they passed was visible to the children sitting cramped in the back of the truck. They soon became terribly hungry, for they had eaten nothing since breakfast, and Black Michael was apparently immune to hunger, though he occasionally took mouthfuls out of a small wooden keg which he carried beside him under the seat. It was getting near sundown when, a little way south of an old abbey which stood alone beside a river, Black Michael stopped the truck and told them they could get down.

" 'Tis only a mile or so more before you reach Cashel," he said, "and I've come far out of my way already to bring ye here. Keep on walking along this road, and maybe ye'll find them ye seek as ye come near to the Rock."

The children thanked him as he pulled the truck round to take a country lane that doubled back towards the north. Once more they found themselves alone upon the road. The country was no longer flat, for behind them there were high mountains whilst immediately in front a great rock rose steeply out of the plain, apparently barring their way. Though they were on a main road, they passed only the smallest of villages, and in none of them was there anything approaching a baker's shop where they might have bought a few cakes with the little silver in Dominic's pocket. The road stretched on and on, the rock seeming to grow no nearer, whilst their way passed through a landscape that grew ever wilder and more desolate.

At last, in a stony gorge through which the road narrowed, their eyes lighted upon two figures who were occupying the middle of the road; not full-sized figures, the children were glad to see, but two boys of exactly the same height and perhaps a couple of years older than themselves who, with the lanky awkward grace of their kind, were cuffing each other good-humoredly on the road.

By tacit consent Dominic and Josephine hastened their pace in order to come up with them, but before they had done so a large green bus filled with passengers came roaring up from behind. At the sound of the bus the two broke off their play and scattered clumsily, their hands stretched out on either side as though groping for something in the dark. As soon as the bus had passed, Dominic and Josephine ranged alongside of these two and realized almost immediately two facts, that these boys actually were what they themselves had often been mistaken for, identical twins, and that both were blind.

Whilst Dominic and Josephine were debating how to make their presence known without unduly startling them, Yanadick settled the matter for them by running between the two boys and with his lead separating one from the other.

"Begob, what's got me?" exclaimed one boy, tripping up over the lead.

"Holy Mother of God, 'tis the devil himself," cried the other, catching hold of one of Yanadick's shapely horns.

"It's all right, it's only our goat!" the children spoke almost simultaneously.

"And who are you, and where are you coming at all with two horns and a long rope?" asked the one boy, still holding Yanadick by the horn.

"We're two twins just like yourselves," spoke Dominic.

"And we're looking for a caravan that's camped between here and Cashel," added Josephine, feeling somehow that all twins must be bound by some sort of alliance. Nor did it seem that she was far wrong.

"Blessings upon the two of ye then, for it will be our van ye're meaning," exclaimed the boy, holding Yanadick's cord. " 'Tis the only van that we know of between Tur-les and Cashel."

"Then you must be Hogans," cried Dominic and Josephine together, "the very family we've come to find!"

"Hogans indeed, at your service," cried one. "Larry's meself and Tumaus there, my brother, and sure, it must have been a miracle that set ye down on this road, and we coming home from selling song sheets in the market at Tur-les."

"It isn't so very wonderful," Dominic admitted. "You see, Black Michael put us down out of his truck only about three miles away, and he picked us up, oh, ever so far away, because the Green-coated Boy told him he had to bring us to find you. And the Green-coated Boy told us that you and your family travel all the roads of Ireland, and if we went with you, sooner or later you'd bring us to our home, us and this billy-goat he gave us."

"Oh, the Green-coated Boy is friends with all of us," Tumaus answered, "and when our mam comes to know that 'tis he that sent you to us, sure it's the glad woman she'll be to bid you welcome, you and your goat as well, for all he's after throwing me on the road. Tell out your names now, so we shall know who to tell her has come?"

Dominic and Josephine told their names, and the four children set out together on the road with the goat Yanadick tripping beside them on his lead.

Nor did they fail to beguile the way in conversation, so that however many miles still lay between them and Cashel of the Kings, it seemed no more than the "mile or so" that Black Michael had promised them. They approached the Rock of Cashel just as the yellow light of evening had golded

its cathedrals, banqueting halls and palaces until it seemed
to the children that the rock wore a veritable crown of gold.
And in the meadows at its foot hung a row of golden garments drying in the setting sun, and behind them a green
caravan, and in the doorway to it a woman and a young
man sitting side by side peeling golden potatoes. The woman
wore a black shade over her eyes and by the side of the young
man a pair of crutches lay ranged. To him Dominic gave a
long look and then, "Why, Miley!" he cried.

CHAPTER XVI

The Blind Musicians

Josephine looked in Dominic's astonished countenance
and then across at the young man so addressed; even the
woman lifted her shaded face and turned it in the direction of Dominic's voice and then to the lad beside her to hear
how he would answer.

"Miley!" Dominic repeated, "whatever are you doing here?"

"And why wouldn't I be here, sitting on my own sister's
doorstep?" asked Miley blandly. "And it's yourself, I'm
thinking, is the lad to be asking such a question and you that
should be feeding your goat in a field seven counties away,
and a goat that's changed its color an' all since the day I
last saw it!"

"What would you expect?" asked Dominic. "Wasn't it you
told me where to look for a Prince of Pucks to mate with our
white nanny? And didn't you go then to the place of the
Green-coated Boy, 'down the river and over the hill,' and
tell him of the wonderful white nanny you'd seen? Of course
we had to set out to find him, and if you'd given us a few
more directions we might have been here days ago! But
we're terribly grateful to you really," he added, "because
Yanadick is even better than we'd imagined, and now that
it's all turned out so well, all we want to do is to go back
home as quickly as we can. The Green-coated Boy was sure
you'd help us, and so we've come all the way here in Black
Michael's truck on purpose to find you."

"Holy Mary, bless the boy!" exclaimed Kathleen Hogan, for she it was. "Is it true, Miley, what he's after telling us? If 'tis so, then why wouldn't the both of them and the goat be coming with us and we taking the road into the north in one week's time or less?"

"Why wouldn't we indeed, sister?" Miley answered, "but that ye've promised these two young ones that before you take that road we will go together to Puck Fair, and from that promise neither they nor I will set you free."

"You did so, Mam," the Hogan twins spoke with one voice. "The time you learnt us to sing, 'twas yourself that said it. We should go to Puck Fair the way all the grand folks in the market place should hear us, and the streets clinking wid silver coins for the picking up!"

"I said so indeed," their mother answered. "I gave them my pledge that should be their reward, the Lord strike me one if I should deceive them! And indeed we would have but to cross the Golden Vale and we should be at Puck Fair before they'd gathered in the harvest. And I'm thinking we should be back in Carrick the very time the great doctor does be travelling that way himself. And then maybe there will be a marvel waiting for Kathleen Hogan, the blind harpist of Cashel!"

She passed her fingers over the shade covering her eyes as though they were itching to tear it off and then, sighing, addressed herself again to the task of peeling potatoes.

"Let me peel them for you," said Josephine, taking the knife out of her hand. "I love peeling potatoes."

For a moment Dominic regarded her with raised eyebrows and then gave vent to something resembling a giggle, but Josephine pretended not to notice him.

"There's just one thing," she said. "We really meant to get home before there was time for our parents to hear from Uncle Theo that we'd run away. You see, they might be wondering what had become of us."

"Could you maybe write them a letter?" the blind woman suggested. "Ye'll get writing paper at the shop that sells

newspapers in the town. Wait now, and I'll bring ye a
stamp."

She vanished into the caravan whilst the two children with
Miley finished peeling the large basinful of potatoes, which
they hung in the pot oven over the fire.

"Sure, 'tis a penance to see them doing such a thing with
never an eye between the lot of them but what grows on the
potatoes," Miley said. "Since her man Larry was taken—
him that played on the pipes—I'm with her more often than
not, helping her with this thing or that."

"We could help her too," cried Dominic. "We could cook
their dinners and fetch the water and bring in sticks for the
fire. . . ."

"Oh, and we've learnt to do much cleverer things than
that," exclaimed Josephine. "We can make soda bread, and
churn milk into butter, and make cheese—all things I simply
adore doing!"

Dominic laughed outright in her face. "Well, it all depends," he remarked sagely. At which moment Kathleen
Hogan returned with a stamp and a few coppers for a loaf of
bread.

It seemed like going shopping in Jerusalem the Golden,
thought Josephine. Above their heads the rock towered, its
fairy pinnacles and flying buttresses in the overspreading
yellow light looking as though they had been washed in gold.
So beautiful were the postcards of this fairy town that they
found in the newspaper shop that they bought two, one for
each parent, telling them that they were staying in a town
built of a golden stone, where they were living with some
blind musicians. That they were all very nice and that they
were taking them in their caravan to Puck Fair, and after
that they would be home again with their goat Yanadick
very soon.

The following morning when they awoke, it was raining
and the sky had turned a silvery grey. So, unfortunately, had
the Rock of Cashel, with an appearance a little less magical,

though it could never be anything less than astounding. So in the week that followed they spent many hours wandering amidst its ancient buildings, its romantic chapel and roofless cathedral, its round tower and its mysterious Coronation Stone etched with the journeys of the sun. Between these expeditions and the performance of the daily chores of the caravan, their days passed very quickly, but it was to the evenings that the children looked forward with the happiest anticipations. Then, with a fine supper of stewed rabbit or trout inside them and a great camp fire in front, they would listen to Kathleen the harpist and her brother Miley, playing

their instruments together, or, to vary the entertainment, the twins, Larry and Tumaus, would sing to them or dance a double jig or, best of all, Miley would put away his fiddle and tell them a story of the days when Cashel had a king indeed and the blind Hogans were his hereditary bards. Afterwards, a very near second to sleeping out of doors, Dominic would join Miley and the twins in the tent whilst Josephine shared the caravan with Kathleen. In a very short time it seemed as though they had known each other for years.

On the day before they were to start for Puck Fair, Kathleen announced that she was to have a grand washing day, and Dominic was dressed in an old coat and trousers belonging to the twins whilst Josephine was simply wrapped in a black shawl and left beside the caravan stove till her clothes were ready for her. Even their heads were washed and combed, after which Kathleen braided first her own dark hair and then Josephine's. Larry, Tumaus and Dominic were given threepence each to go to the barber's, whence they returned with tales even more striking than Miley's.

"Mam, they say down at Puck Fair they does be catching an old billy-goat off the mountains and hauling him up by the horns higher than the cathedral here, and leaving him there three days, the poor baste!"

"And Mam, they say 'tis all to celebrate the day the wild goats came down from the mountains and ran through the town to give the folk warning that the redcoats was behind them, coming with fire and sword to light up the town, and so the people was saved."

"Holy Mary, 'twill be a grand sight whichever way it is," said Kathleen, not quite following the tale. "And will ye now take the auld harse to the forge, for I misdoubt the sound of his off-hind shoe, and 'tis a far journey before us!"

And so it turned out to be, a far journey but a merry one, the new mode of life delighting the children, over country where every cloud seemed to be hiding a mountain-top

higher than any they had known. Mostly whilst Kathleen drove, with Miley whistling along beside the horse, the children and the goat walked or trotted behind, the blind Hogans following closely the sound of the wheels.

If it chanced that at nightfall they arrived on the outskirts of some little town, the Hogan twins would set out, usually followed by Dominic and Josephine, and, standing at a street corner, would sing together some old song from their mother's repertoire, and as their voices were true and the words came clearly, they would soon attract a little audience ready to drop a few coppers into the cap which Dominic held ready to pass round. If Miley and his fiddle were with them, the song would be followed by a step dance which brought in more coppers still.

"You make me feel quite ashamed," Dominic protested one evening very near the end of their journey. "Here are you two bringing in a whole capful of coppers every time you go out, and Josephine and I don't contribute a brass farthing to help with the housekeeping, and yet I sometimes think we eat more than the rest of you put together!"

"And you to say so after collecting a big sackful of sticks and branches for the fire tonight, and your sister so skilful at lighting it," cried Tumaus, "and twenty dozen other things as well. Only yesterday our mam was telling us yours was the eyes for all the jobs Larry and her and me was for doing in the dark, God helping us."

"But did ye not hear her, Tumaus," cried his brother; "did ye not hear what she was telling then? The dark, she said, was never so dark as it was once in the little crack of light the shade lets through. It is getting brighter with every day that dawns!"

"Praise be to God, and she to have eyes for the three of us!" cried Tumaus. "Eh, now, would that not be the wonder of the world? But tell me now, Dominic, have we not money enough in the cap to buy us a bit of bacon to go in with the rabbit that Miley snared for our supper? I think there will surely be a store somewhere in this town where you could find such a thing, and will that not be the grand surprise on our mam and Josephine?"

Yes, Dominic remembered passing a store as they came into the town, with its name, O'Sullivan's Store, painted in red letters over the doorway. It was still open, a pleasant smell of bacon, cheese and tarred string permeating the atmosphere which would soon, however, be charged with the smell of spirits by the look of several thirsty men further down the long counter. They were grouped around a man of

medium height whose age Dominic was unable to guess, who wore a pair of patched riding breeches, a shabby fawn hacking coat, worn riding boots and a red spotted stock round his neck which accorded well with a nose that was long, narrow and red at the tip. On his head, at a rakish angle, was poised a battered ring-master's hat.

He had just astonished the small audience in the shop by changing an egg into a lemon when his eye fell upon Dominic standing in the shadows by the door.

"Perhaps that young gentleman would care to assist me," he said, intimating Dominic, who blushed. "He has an intelligent face. Meantime another round, I think, gentlemen."

The professor of conjuring, if such he was, nodded to the barman and more porter was produced to gladden the hearts of his audience while the professor explained that the trick he was about to show them had been performed by only one other man, who had since died in Prague.

He drew a five-pound note from his pocket, passed it round the awestruck assembly and then, holding it delicately between the tips of his fingers, he lit a match and burnt it to a fine ash.

"Now sir," he said, addressing Dominic, "perhaps you will oblige us by looking in your left-hand coat pocket?"

Dominic produced a handful of cake crumbs, the stump of a pencil, his penknife and finally handed over the note, folded up very small.

Amid the general astonishment the professor picked up his Malacca cane and with a flourish of his hat departed before the landlord realized that the drinks had not been paid for.

When at last Dominic was served with his bacon, Mr. O'Sullivan treated him with marked disapproval, evidently suspecting him of complicity in the final trick. When they arrived back at the caravan and Josephine unwrapped the bacon, it turned out that it was both mouldy and rusty.

Meanwhile Dominic found the Hogan twins when he rejoined them agog with some important news. "Have ye heard there's to be a circus at the Fair?" Tumaus exclaimed. "All the folks was talking of it as we waited by the cross."

"Yes so," added Larry, "and there was a lady—young she seemed, had seen it coming down the road from Killarney. There was a lion in one cage, and a menagerie in another, and an elephant walking along the road was one of the world's wonders, with a tail and a pair of eyes at each end of him!"

"And there was pictures, she told us, on the caravan," Larry took up the tale, "of a fairy jumping through a paper hoop, and a magician with a wand, and he was raising up a beautiful lady out of a hat with one hand, and turning a rabbit into an egg with the other!"

"Oho," said Dominic, "and did he set fire to one five-pound note, find another one in some mug's pocket, and yet go off without paying for his drinks? Then I met him just now where I went to buy the bacon." And Dominic related his adventure.

"They'll surely be going to Puck Fair," said Kathleen when she heard of Dominic's encounter with the conjurer. "And let you now take warning of what happens to any children or poor simple folk that hearkens to their blarney. They'll talk ye into buying a gold watch and it not even of silver, or a cure for piles maybe that is nothing but a red drench for a cow. Their customs is not our customs, nor their people anything but strangers and foreigners in Ireland. Leave them be if ye should find them at the Fair, for it's nothing but tricks and cheating ye'll get out of such as they."

"But Mam," pleaded Tumaus, "it's never the elephant nor the menagerie will cheat us. Let Larry and me but make enough by our singing, and the four of us will go and see the animals for ourselves, and you to stay in the caravan if ye have such dread of the circus folk."

"Let you make your money first by your songs," Kathleen laughed gently. "Maybe the people of the Fair will be too much taken up with drinking and with playing of cards to pay attention to ye at all."

THE BLIND MUSICIANS

Josephine looked across at the face beneath the shadowed eyes, the sad serenity of the mouth, the experience and wisdom that must surely lie behind the shade. It was a face she had come to trust. She was less sure now that she wanted to go to Puck Fair.

"We might go and look at them anyhow," said Dominic. A flicker of light seemed to pass over his face. "Perhaps they might give me a job," he added.

Had Dominic had one of his good ideas?

CHAPTER XVII

The Circus

It was very early next morning, the sun not yet risen, when they heard the song of the Elephant Man, the Mahout, coming from far away down the road; nothing but that filling the still air with its odd risings and fallings, its long-drawn-out wordless line, more of a chant than a song. Six faces appeared almost instantly at the tent opening and the door of the caravan; six faces of which to only three were the fantastic beast and his strange rider visible; foreigners indeed they seemed on the small Irish road.

Slowly and in absolute silence except for the high nasal singing voice, they approached, passed and as slowly disappeared down the road, only the thin line of distant song bearing witness to their passing.

Only then did the children break the silence after their various fashions, the Hogan twins as eager for the descriptive picture which Miley and Dominic were as eager to give, Josephine, turning to the blind woman beside her with a sigh of wonder. "How I wish," she breathed, "I could get to know an elephant really well!"

"But I'm thinking we'll find him tonight at the Fair," answered Kathleen. "It's that way the road leads, and 'tis not far from the fairground to the place where the caravans does be pulling in."

"Will there be other caravans as well as ours then?" asked Josephine.

"A whole row of them spread out beyond the bridge and beside the river," Kathleen replied. "Nothing but tinkers they is, giddy with drink after the first day, but no harm in them except to fritter your money away listening to their foolish fortune-telling, in the cards, and in the tea-leaves and in the crystal. Shadow a bit of sense can I see in becoming acquainted with the future, if ye cannot alter it. Faith, 'tis nothing but a discouragement! But come now, Josephine, 'tis time we was cooking that bit of bacon your brother brought in last night, for it's early we must be on the road and we to come to Puck Fair before darkness."

It was even as Kathleen had said and the circus was there before them. Going down the hill from the market place, where the high platform for the Puck was already set up, they

came upon a great noise of hammering, and a break in the houses showed the Big Top away to the left, the roundabout close beside it, and a multitude of tents and caravans all pricked out with the scarlet banners and red and white trappings of the typical fairground. No sooner had Miley parked the caravan behind the half-dozen others that had already arrived than Dominic and Josephine set off to gaze and gape at the strange sights of the circus, its astounding people and all the multifarious activities in which they were engaged. But Kathleen Hogan, calling Larry and Tumaus to her side, set them to the weaving of little baskets made of rushes, which they hoped to sell filled with heather to the visitors at the Fair.

The next day, although the Gathering was several days distant, the flags began to go up in all quarters of the town, whilst across the road, leading to the market place, a great white banner hung on which was inscribed in Irish and English the words "Ten thousand welcomes to all who come" in great letters of red.

The sun shone merrily down upon all this, making the circus look like some elaborate toy turned to life by an enchanter, or like a colored illustration in a book of fairytales. Dominic and Josephine could not keep away, but just as they were setting out for a second visit, by daylight, Kathleen called to Josephine to say they had better make use of the fine shiny day to do some washing, if they had a mind to look clean and self-respecting children the time the Fair began.

So Dominic stayed to help them that they might be ready the quicker, and soon Josephine was hanging a row of medium-sized shirts on a line in the field behind the caravan whilst Dominic handed her the pegs, when a young man with a missing front tooth and long hair sticking out from under his cloth cap came across to them from the field which backed on to the fairground.

"Will you ask your mother if she can do any washing for us?" he said, addressing Josephine.

"But we haven't got a mother. We don't live here; we're only here because of Puck Fair," Josephine told him.

"Indeed, and I'm an orphan myself," said the young man. They recognized him now as Corky, the circus mechanic who had sung "By Killarney's Lakes and Fells" so feelingly whilst setting up the roundabout the previous evening. "I've got a guardian though," he went on. "A very fine gentleman he is. He lives at 72 Henry Street, Cork. I write to him once a month; leastways, whenever I can get someone to do the writing for me, for I'm not much of a hand at the bookwork."

"Oh, we've got a guardian too," Dominic volunteered, "but we don't like him much. . . . At least, he isn't bad, but we've left him for one reason or another and now we're looking for work."

"Looking for work, are you? Hi, Curly, Otto!" Corky called over his shoulder to two young men who now appeared; a jolly-looking fat man and a sad-seeming dark one with a long face and enormous rather prominent black eyes. "These two kiddoes are looking for work. I'm telling you," he was beginning, turning back to Dominic. "The boss is a hard man. . . ."

"Undoubtedly two talented young artists seeking an opportunity to express their talents. I think we have met before," said an educated voice from behind, and a cloud seemed to fall upon the group. Dominic, aware of a smell of whiskey, turned about and encountered again the gaze of the great Professor Salomon the conjurer. "But this time there are two of you—twins if I'm not mistaken," the professor continued, looking from Dominic to Josephine and back again. "A very well-matched pigeon pair. Now, what sort of work were you thinking of?"

"Oh, anything at all, sir," replied Dominic, determined to make a good impression, "so long as we can make a little money, to help pay for our keep."

"A very laudable ambition!" commented the professor. "And of course we pay our staff generously, though even if we did not, they would be proud to work in Salomon's circus, isn't that so, boys?" He turned to the three young men, who cleared their throats and shifted their weight from one foot to the other. Salomon continued to eye Dominic and Josephine, his head a little thrown back, his eyes half-closed. A smile began to appear beneath the small dark moustache.

"We have an elephant in our circus," he began, "a bear, a psychological pig and a mathematical horse. We have two clowns—you see them before you!" he indicated Curly and Otto; "an equestrienne, but she is away in hospital with measles; and then, of course, there is Madame Salomon, who is a host in herself—or a hostess, perhaps I should say." He laughed facetiously and then made an impressive pause. "But the one thing we have not, and never have had is—a pair of Siamese twins."

"But we aren't Siamese twins," Josephine pointed out immediately. "We aren't even identical twins, which are always either both boys or both girls. But we have some identical twins in our caravan; both boys and exactly alike, and I expect. . . ."

"But Dominic took her up. "I don't expect their mother would let them come," he said. "And anyway, they are both blind. But what exactly were you thinking of, sir?"

"I can see in my mind," said the professor rather mysteriously and still keeping his eyes half-shut, "a large sack, with two holes in it large enough to accommodate a pair of legs each. And I believe that if the children inside the sack were tied firmly together, there would be nothing at all to show that they were not—Salomon's Siamese Twins!"

He broke into a peal of triumphant laughter which Dominic echoed, but Josephine looked dubious. "But wouldn't that be deceiving the public?" she asked doubtfully; "taking their money on false pretences, committing a crime almost?" She gave the professor a very square look.

"A crime? How preposterous!" Salomon exclaimed. "You are twins, aren't you?—and two twins joined together are Siamese twins. How they are joined is quite immaterial."

Josephine was silent. "Besides," Dominic urged her, "think what a lot of money we'd bring back to the Hogans at night! Perhaps we could pay for all the days they've kept us for already."

It certainly seemed an important point.

"Have you ever run a three-legged race together?" the professor asked them.

"Oh yes," both children cried, suddenly brightening. "At Josephine's school sports. We were awfully good. We won a prize!" added Dominic.

This seemed to clinch matters. "Well, go and practise it now," said the professor, looking very gratified. "Come for an interview with Madame Salomon at the same time tomorrow morning, and we'll see what we can make of you."

158

THE CIRCUS

All the rest of that day and at any time when they were not wanted in the caravan, Dominic and Josephine practised their steps. In the patch of field behind the caravan there was ample space for them to work up to quite a climax of three-legged speed, and at last they found they could keep in step with no handkerchief to do the attaching. Then they turned to dancing, and, a loose cord round their middles, found they could achieve quite a reasonable waltz step. Beside them Larry and Tumaus, ambitious artists too, were practising their steps for the double jig they intended to dance in the competition on the day of the Gathering, whilst Yanadick, perhaps the greatest artist of them all, excited at such goings-on, executed a series of frolicking caprioles of his own.

CHAPTER XVIII

Otto and Orpine

To Kathleen, Dominic and Josephine decided that they would say as little as possible of their new activities. Time enough, Dominic thought, when they brought her their first capful of coins to tell her how they had been earned. For the present, they had said that they were doing odd jobs for the circus people, and although she made it evident that she could not approve, she made no attempt to sever their connection with a world she so much mistrusted. As the days before the Fair succeeded each other, more and more of their time was spent in the vicinity of the Big Top. Their interview with Madame Salomon had been entirely successful. She was a heavily built Levantine, considerably older than the professor, who had, rumor had it—and rumor had many tongues in the circus—married the professor when her first husband, the owner of the menagerie in Belgrade, was eaten by a bear.

"Not the *same* bear?" cried Josephine in horror, eyeing the very elderly bear cracking bones in a corner of his cage, who was said to have lived on from the circus's earliest days.

"Aw, I do not think he can be the same," Otto answered. "Of course it may be—a sort of insurance against husbands, but in any case, not the same bones."

Otto, they learnt, was the nephew of Madame Salomon, whom he greatly resembled in that you might have met either of them on an icon. The professor, who had spent much of his youth drifting about the world, had fallen in with the circus in Belgrade and joined it in a moment of discouragement. The menagerie had sadly declined since those days, and the Salomons were extremely anxious to recruit new talent in both sorts for their circus. Mazeppa the equestrienne was the only child of their marriage, and her defection to a hospital in Cork left a sad blank in the program, and this the professor was now planning to fill with Salomon's Siamese Twins.

"Perhaps you would like to look after the pony," he suggested next. "My daughter always did, and the poor creature misses her."

"Oh, we should love that!" Josephine cried. "Perhaps you could teach us to ride?"

"I can see no reason why I should not," said the professor, lighting a cigarette. "Then you could take Mazeppa's place the next time she falls ill."

Josephine thought this sounded very exciting. She tried to imagine herself as the fairy on the poster, jumping through a paper hoop with a silver star on her forehead. Otto was holding the hoop.

Though they liked Corky, who could do anything with machinery, and Curly, the fat clown who was always ready to make them laugh, Otto was by far their favorite of all the circus folk. Him they followed like dogs through all the multifarious jobs of "getting ready for the show." He it was who was detailed to contrive the sack and put the Siamese Twins through their rehearsal and then, in the capacity of critic, to give them a demonstration of what was wrong with their performance, for he was an admirable mimic. But always, even though he had been in the gayest spirits a moment before, Otto's face when in repose assumed an expression so downcast that the children were haunted by its deep melancholy.

Dominic taxed him with it. "Otto, why do you always look so glum?" he asked. "You make other people laugh; why don't you make yourself laugh, Otto, as well?"

"Laugh? Otto?" said the clown. "What for should Otto laugh? Life is sad; he is lonely, and over here it rains always. In Belgrade it is different. The sun shines; even the cats laugh in Belgrade. In America it is different too. In America are friends; a sister. One day Otto shall go to them. He will work; he will be a rich man. Then he will laugh!"

"I suppose he wishes he had never left Belgrade," was Josephine's comment afterwards. "I don't think he likes his aunt and the professor much, do you?"

"I'm perfectly certain he doesn't," answered Dominic with decision. "Look at the way they fag him all the time! I wonder he doesn't run away, like us!"

"I suppose he'd only be lonelier than ever," said Josephine. Let's go and find Tumaus and Larry and take them along to the circus. I'm sure they'll laugh at him and love him. I expect they'll be at MacDonagh's."

They made their way to MacDonagh's, a pub where the Hogan twins were well known, and there, sure enough, were Tumaus and Larry standing in the entrance to the bar singing "The Flight of the Earls" to an audience consisting mainly of tinkers. These people were by now arriving in flocks, their barrel-shaped vans ranged one behind the other resembling nothing so much as a great serpent winding its way into the town. Outside a light rain was falling, but Tumaus and Larry appeared to be hesitating, standing half-in and half-out of the doorway, afraid perhaps that Mr. MacDonagh might find their presence unwelcome.

"Come in then, come in out of the wet!" a young kind voice had just addressed them. "I told ye before not to stay outside."

The voice belonged to Orpine, Mr. MacDonagh's daughter, and at its bidding Tumaus and Larry passed inside and were soon munching a rough tough, a large over-baked cake stuffed sparsely with currants and raisins. They were talking to a blue-eyed girl who looked as if she might have been crying but whose face regained its composure as she chatted with the Hogan twins. At the sight of Dominic and Josephine,

"Holy Saints in Heaven," she exclaimed, "is it nothing but twins the tinkers does be breeding? Come in, the both of yous. There's a rough tough for each of ye as well, but ate it quickly now, before my father is back from his decorating."

Hardly had they cleared up the last crumbs before Mr. MacDonagh walked in. The girl cast apprehensive glances in his direction but at first her father's mind had room for nothing but the flags and green boughs that he and his cronies had been fixing to the scaffolding and platform of the Puck's throne outside. "Sixty feet high, I'm telling you, and not an inch less! 'Tis a steady head that one will need, the sorra he will, or his days of roaming the mountains is over. Why, what have we here?" he exclaimed as his eyes took in the extremely youthful appearance of his *clientèle.*

"Arrah, it's just some poor children come in to liven the folks with a song. Sing up now you, Larry, Tumaus. Sure 'The Flight of the Earls' is known to all here."

Nothing loth, the Hogan twins piped up together:

> *Beside the camp fire's fitful blaze,*
> *Amid the forest drear,*
> *I picture in the dying rays*
> *The home to me so dear.*
> *The lowly cot, the leaping stream,*
> *The spire upon the hill,*
> *I see them as I lie and dream;*
> *My heart is with them still.*

Mr. MacDonagh nodded his head indulgently in time with the music. But when Larry came to handing his cap round, his audience of tinkers shuffled away or shook their heads, only one or two of the "regulars" slipping in a copper or two, "for the sake of auld Ireland."

"Faith, they will be saving their money for the Fair," said the landlord, "and it's not songs they will be spending it on then, I'm thinking! And you two," he went on, turning to Dominic and Josephine, "Ye're singers too maybe, or is it step-dancing is your skill?"

"No, sir," Dominic answered. "We can't sing and we don't dance, but we belong to the circus and the opening day is tomorrow, so we hope to entertain you there."

A spasm of anger crossed Mr. MacDonagh's face. "May I be destroyed first," he exclaimed, "before I spend good money on that trash! Now, out of this, all of yous, and let decent folk come in. It's no space we have here for the likes of you bringing in the mud and the menagerie droppings of that place on the feet of you. Be off, I say!"

The four children, not a little crestfallen, quickly disappeared but Josephine, turning her head, caught a smile from the blue eyes as the lips dumbly formed the words, "Come back!"

"That was Orpine, old John MacDonagh's daughter," explained Tumaus as soon as they were outside.

"Is it not a shame an' all the way he treats her?" said his brother, "and she the loveliest girl in all the town!"

"Yes, I think she's beautiful," cried Josephine, mistaking his meaning and forgetting that he could not see. "But why had she been crying when we came in?"

"Was she so?" asked Larry, his own face clouding over. "But there, shadow a bit I know of the things girls cries for!"

"Maybe you'd cry," his brother hazarded, "if ye had a da as cross as hers is."

"He seemed pretty cross with the circus people," Dominic commented. "I'd better not have said we had anything to do with them."

"And besides that," Josephine added, "I don't think we ought to say too much about belonging to the circus when we're supposed to be Siamese Twins. Just think if somebody were to stand up in the audience and say they'd seen us walking about perfectly separate. Why, they might ask for their money back!"

The prospect was most alarming and Dominic promised to be more guarded in future.

"But Orpine wasn't angry with us," he said. "Didn't she smile at you, Josephine, just as we were coming away?"

"She said, 'Come back!' " said Josephine, her eyes shining. "Let's go back tomorrow and see if we can't cheer her up. Why shouldn't we take her out for a picnic and get Corky and Curly and Otto to come too, to make her laugh?"

"I don't know about Otto," Dominic objected; "he's often frightfully sad himself. He might be a regular wet blanket!"

Josephine considered it. "I don't think Otto would be sad at a party," she said then. "Just think how he can make people laugh when he really tries to! Besides, if he's sad, we ought to try to cheer him up as well. We'll get Kathleen and Miley to bring their instruments, and with them playing and

Tumaus and Larry dancing, the party will go like anything, you'll see!"

So the next morning, which was Saturday, they all went back to MacDonagh's and when they had watched himself go off down the road that led to the bridge, they stole into the bar which appeared to be quite empty until, looking through an open door leading into a room behind, they saw Orpine seated on the hearthrug, her elbows on a chair, her head buried in her arms.

Josephine ran forward and put her arm round the girl. "Dear Orpine, don't cry like that," she said, feeling almost like crying herself. "We've come to help you."

Orpine shook her head, as though at her own goings on, held her breath for a few moments to stay her sobs and then wiped her eyes. " 'Tis nothing," she said then. " 'Tis just . . . the world . . . is such a lonesome place!"

The children looked at each other over her head, their eyes full of consternation. "It's just what Otto said," Dominic whispered. "I never knew grown-ups went on about it so."

"Listen to me, Orpine," said Josephine. "We're going to have a party on purpose to cheer you up—a sort of picnic with some nice friends of ours, with music and dancing. Can you come tonight? It's our last free evening before the show begins tomorrow. Oh, do say you can come!"

Orpine wiped her swollen eyes, gave a watery smile. "Sure it's dear children that you are," she said, "to trouble your heads about poor Orpine. Go away now, for if my father comes to find there's circus children been here, he'll murder the lot of ye."

"Will you come then?" urged Dominic. "We'll come and fetch you about six o'clock."

"Wait now," Orpine considered. " 'Tis the evening before the Fair begins. My father will be closing the shop and going with the other men to the mountains to catch the Puck. We could be gone and come back again and he still searching the mountains for the poor beast."

"Six o'clock then, tonight, we'll be here," said Dominic. "Don't forget."

There was to be a final rehearsal in the Big Top that afternoon so the children had a busy day. They began by seeking Miley's co-operation.

Miley was always one for a party and he knew besides the very place, he said, where such a *cailey*[1] could be held; a distant glen where the old way across the mountains ran before they built the new road. He himself, he announced, would be responsible for the drinks and the music for the dancing. Even Kathleen, hearing that the children's favorite Orpine was sad and needed to be cheered, agreed to bring her harp and lift their hearts with song. Besides that, she had in her cupboard a raisin cake and a barm brac; decidedly good cheer in that too, the children considered. They themselves with the last of Dominic's shillings bought some oranges, some bananas and two bottles of fizzy lemonade. Then, before the rehearsal began, they sought out Corky, Curly and Otto.

But Corky had found a girl friend who had promised to help him with the letter to his guardian, now somewhat overdue. Tonight was her evening out, and he had arranged to go and fetch her from the house where she worked as soon as the rehearsal was over. Vainly did Dominic proffer his own help there and then, boasting of his prowess in spelling.

"It's not an educated letter he will be looking for at all," Corky objected. "And who are you, anyway, to be writing a nice friendly letter to a man's guardian when you've given your own guardian the slip and come away with never a word said, by your own telling? No, it's a nice sweet girl will write me my letter, and when he reads all the loving messages at the end, it will, maybe, put it into his head to send me a postal order for fifteen shillings, as he did last time, by the very next post."

Nor did they fare better with Curly. His feet were destroying him, he said, and before the show opened tomorrow he

[1] Music party.

had promised himself a clear evening with Dr. Keen's One Night Corn Cure. "How will I go chasing Otto all around the ring and he after hitting me on the nob with a plank when I'm ready to cry out in torment every step I take? No, 'tis no dancing in the glen is my aspiration; just plenty of hot water and me weight off me feet."

So in the end it was Otto alone who accepted their kind invitation to a party with music, dancing and refreshments. And his contribution was perhaps the most valuable of all, for it included not only thick ham sandwiches and chocolates from Miss Slattery's, the baker and confectioner, but the loan of a vehicle in which, under Miley's guidance, the caravan horse should convey hosts and guests to the glen in the mountains.

For once, Orpine did not look as though she had been crying. With sparkling looks and flushed cheeks she was waiting at the door to greet them.

"This is Orpine," the children said, proud of their new friend, and Otto rose to help her to climb into the cart. As he handed her to the seat between himself and Kathleen they looked at each other quickly and laughed, before Orpine turned to Kathleen and began to talk to her about Larry and Tumaus. The party seemed to be going very well, and the talk and laughter did not cease until the end of the journey.

By this time they were deep into the heart of the mountains, following the old green road that led to the lakes. All about them great mountains, the highest peaks in Ireland, raised their pointed heads, whilst on their hoary shoulders, to the children's delight, the wild goats clambered and hopped like fleas.

"If only Yanadick were here . . ." cried Josephine.

"We'd never catch him again!" Dominic finished for her, and she wondered what means Orpine's father used to attract and capture a creature so wild.

"Faith, it's often the same old goat they takes, year after year," the girl told her. "I think the old fella likes it. He's

169

crowned, do you see, with a crown of gold to show him for the best Puck of the year. It's no marvel he lives on vanity alone!"

At a point where a fainter smaller path crossed the old way diagonally, they pulled up, for Miley had seen something. One of the old platforms set up for cross-road dancing was still in place, rotting at the edges but sound still in the middle. Here too the glen had narrowed, reefs of stone rising out of the turf which could be used as seats by onlookers and musicians. They alighted and spread their feast, and so for a short while there was silence, for they had fasted since noon.

It was into the midst of this silence, after a brief noise of wheels, that the wedding party made its entrance, three horse-drawn flies appearing down the diagonal path, one of which came to a halt in close proximity to the party already in possession.

Josephine clutched Dominic. "Look, Dominic, just look what's getting out!"

Very slowly a couple of sticks were poked out of the cab and prodded into the soft turf. Then a pair of feet clad in grey worsted stockings followed them, and finally an ancient dame, her head and shoulders swathed in a black shawl, slowly let herself down backwards out of the cab.

"Heaven defend me if it isn't a wedding party!" cried Orpine as a girl in white and a young man with much-anointed hair alighted from the foremost cab.

"Then do you think this one is the bad fairy they forgot to invite to the wedding?" suggested Josephine.

"No, I think she's just an old trout," Dominic rejoined, refusing to follow the path of romance. "But look, there's somebody with her."

"Oh, what a pretty girl!" cried Josephine. "How old do you think she is?"

"Anywhere between you and Orpine," Dominic hazarded. "But see who's getting out of the last cab."

It was indeed the priest who had performed the ceremony. His vehicle had hardly pulled up before he was out of it inspecting the dancing floor. Small, wizened and elvish, one had only to watch his quicksilver movements to know him where the dance was concerned for the master of ceremonies.

He looked around. "But the Boy is not here!" he exclaimed. "I thought he would surely be here before us."

Every one seemed a little disquieted by this. Dominic and Josephine exchanged glances whilst Kathleen turned her head towards the speaker, listening intently for what should come next.

The old woman spoke. "Lave'm be," she said. "He's maybe walking the hills to us this very moment."

All eyes were turned to the hills, but nothing was seen there but the gambolling goats. Kathleen half-rose to her feet.

"Do I hear the voice of Molly O'Shane?" she asked.

" 'Twas I, Molly O'Shane, that spake," the old woman replied, "and I think the voice that questions is the voice of Kathleen Hogan the harpist. And are these the twin sons of my Larry? A blessing from God on ye, my bright loves." She kissed Tumaus and Larry, dropping a stick as she did so. It was replaced in her hand by the young girl, her companion. "Lead on, Shiela," she addressed the girl. "We shall have no farther to seek for music this night. Let us greet our friends, new and old, and then, in the name of God, let the dance begin!"

Blessings and toasts were in the air. The young couple were cousins, it appeared; grandchildren of old Molly, and Shiela the bridesmaid, was another. The Boy, who seemed to be known to all, guests and hosts alike, had played his pipes at the wedding and now he was gone, and nobody could tell where. No doubt he was straying the mountains amongst the goats, as was his habit. "Maybe," said one, "he'll be caught and put up on the platform in mistake for one of those at tomorrow's doings." But now, cried the priest, they had found music and friends all at the same time, and how could friends pass a wedding day better than in dancing. Too long it was, said he, since there had been dancing feet in the glen.

Indeed Miley was already tuning his fiddle and Kathleen, her head bowed over her harp, was touching its strings. Very soon the bridegroom had led out the bride and the priest followed suit with the bride's mother. Otto and Orpine were already on the floor when the young girl Shiela, who had so captured Josephine's fancy, crossed over to her and took her hand.

"Come out, my heart, and we'll dance together," she cried. It was in vain that Josephine protested that she knew nothing of the Irish dances.

"Yeh, who minds?" the girl exclaimed. "You won't be the first I've learnt to dance in a set. In the country places 'tis the Irish dances still for all of us but in the towns, do you see, where they plays jazzes and all sorts, there isn't one would lose their sweat for an Irish dance. Come out now, 'tis the 'Siege of Ennis' they're playing and it's not hard to follow. Why, here's Kathleen's twins coming with your brother himself."

So Josephine and Dominic, laughing and panting, were pushed this way and that. "No, my soul, you're wrong!" "Arrah, child, go round the other way!" But every one was in high good humor and all the time the music whirled them along, the fiddle frolicking aloft, the harp mellowing it with honeyed chords below till the whole company danced like souls possessed, the priest, the skirts of his cassock tucked up, calling ever on Miley to play still faster.

It was not till the evening shadows began to fall and the glen darkened that the dancers came back to themselves. It was Orpine then, looking at the stars spangling the mountain tops, who said with dismay that she feared her father must have returned home and be seeking her.

Then indeed there was a catching of hobbled horses straying out in the moon shadows, a gathering together of the remnants of the feast, and soon a parting of old friends met together after so long, as the three cabs took the little old roadway through the pass, and Miley and his passengers turned their backs on the mountains and took the green road home.

OTTO AND ORPINE

Just before the party ended Orpine and Otto, who had been whispering together for some time, crossed over to bid the little priest farewell and stayed talking whilst the horses were put in.

"Haven't we given a lovely party?" Josephine whispered to Dominic.

"And if we gave it to cheer those two up, we've certainly succeeded," said he.

"Do you know," she continued, "I almost wondered once if they hadn't met before."

"I know. That look they gave each other in the cart, like people do, and the next thing they say is, "How small the world is!"

"But they didn't say it."

"No, but they laughed!"

CHAPTER XIX

Puck Fair: The Gathering

The first thing that Dominic thought of as he awoke next morning was Puck Fair. This Sunday was the day on which it opened; this was the day on which Salomon's Siamese Twins were to make their début.

Though it was not a very large part they played in the program, he considered it quite an honorable one, for they were to come running in at the head of the parade followed by the mathematical horse and the psychological pig—a procession that culminated with the inscrutable Indian riding his elephant.

Madame Salomon, searching amongst her properties, had come upon two pairs of scarlet vests and tights, once belonging to Mazeppa but long since outgrown. In these, collared and cuffed with gold braid, the twins fancied themselves enormously. Later, when the Indian set the elephant dancing and the old Belgrade bear, balancing a bun on the end of his nose, mounted his stool, the twins too had attained an expertise equal to any of these as they slowly revolved to the tune of "The Blue Danube," which was Madame Salomon's favorite air. Since Madame had cut off Josephine's braids and given Dominic's hair an exactly similar cut, the twins' resemblance to each other was even more striking, and in the intervals of their star turns, they were to be turned into a sort of loose box next door to the mathematical horse where no inquiring visitor to the show could possibly fail to see them.

174

To make doubly sure, however, there was an enormous placard over their heads which bore the legend "Professor Salomon's Siamese Twins captured in Siam during the Late War." Madame Salomon, an expert in make-up, had even given a slight lift to the outside corners of their eyes and eyebrows, which made them feel as if they were quite definitely somebody else.

Dominic was dwelling pleasantly upon this rosy future when he was recalled to the present by a cry from Josephine outside the tent. "Dominic, when did you last see Yanadick? He's gone!"

"I can't think. Yes I can; yesterday evening, before we started for the mountains, I moved him on to some fresh grass."

"Well, he's broken his collar this time and he's gone!" Josephine's tragic face appeared in the opening of the tent. She was holding the broken collar, weakened by much chafing, in her hand.

"That's it," Miley joined in the conversation. "He'll have gone off to the mountains after all the wild black goats." The devil himself knows when ye'll see him back."

But Josephine had an idea. "The Green-coated Boy!" she cried more hopefully. "Do you think he came to see us, and Yanadick followed him?"

"He'd never have whistled him away with never a word said," Miley answered.

"Let's hurry across to the circus," Dominic suggested, "and see if anybody there has seen him. If it's to the mountains he's gone, the nearest way would be across the fairground."

They set off to seek Curly and Corky, but as has already been described, both had been fully occupied during the time in question with their own affairs. But both seemed well satisfied with the way their evening had gone, and were prepared to give their kindest sympathy to the twins in their misfortune.

"Let's go and see old Otto," Corky said. "He may be able to think up something."

They went together to the tent in which Otto lodged, but
he too appeared to have gone, his sleeping-bag neatly folded,
his clown's outfit hanging dejectedly from a peg, all the rest
of Otto appeared to have vanished.

"Crikey, his valise!" cried Corky. "He always had his
shaving tackle and soap laid out on it, and there's the whole
lot gone!"

"Just as if he never meant to come back," added Curly,
"and the show starting today. One of us had better go and
tell the Boss, but I'd liefer it was you than me!"

"Wait a bit," Corky advised. "He can't really have gone.
Why, there's nowhere for him to go! You'll see, he'll come
back in time for the show. Otto always was a rum 'un, but he
was never one for being late."

"Yanadick and Otto both gone," Josephine lamented as
they turned for home. "You'd almost think they'd gone off
together. Whatever shall we do without them? And after last
night, when everything was so lovely!" Josephine seemed
very near to tears.

"And the circus starting today, just when we were going to
earn our livings at last," added Dominic in accents as tragic
as hers. "But if we start hunting for Yanadick now, we're
sure to find someone who's seen him. I think he'd come if
he heard us calling him, and we'd be back before the show
began."

So they started their search cheerfully enough, taking the
road that led out of the town in the direction of the mountains. They knocked at each door they came to, asking for
any news of a stray black goat, but though they received a
variety of replies, not one of them was in the least promising.
The town left behind, they took the nearest road to the mountains, stopping to repeat their question at every house and to
every passer-by they met. But the houses were few and the
passers-by, though many, whether in cars, carts, on bicycles
or afoot, were all eagerly proceeding to the same destination.
There was no doubt that it was Gathering Day at Puck Fair.

PUCK FAIR: THE GATHERING

It was not until they had gone some miles and had reached the first of the foothills that they heard anything hopeful. An old woman, digging potatoes in a roadside field, had seen a black goat not long since, crossing a hill that led towards the higher mountains. "It's on the Reeks you'll find him," she said, "and there may he stay without being led into temptation by the sight of my cabbage garden!"

So they climbed the hill and saw not one goat but many on the next hill southwards. "Of course, he'll have joined the herd," they told each other, and though they had now been walking all morning they set out with new vigor on the track of these goats. But as they approached, the herd withdrew even farther towards the mountains, and so they might have led and the children followed till day turned to night had not Dominic, looking backwards, realized that they were surrounded on all sides by high mountains, that to judge by the position of the sun it must be long past noon, and that they were besides supremely hungry; a hunger they had no means of appeasing.

Sadly then they decided to give up their search for today and return to the circus by the quickest route they could find. Little hope was there now of their rejoining it in time for the opening performance; the début of Salomon's Siamese Twins would have to wait for the evening show, and Dominic wondered how the professor would fill his program if Otto too had failed to reappear. For the moment it was enough that they had to find their way out of this maze of mountains, each pointed cone so much resembling the others; each changing its shape entirely as the children approached it from a new angle. But it was a clear day; the sun helped Dominic's own natural sense of direction and by six o'clock hungry, thirsty and utterly weary, they were approaching the town. Whilst still at some distance from it they could hear the strains of mechanical music and an announcer's amplified voice followed by absolute silence, and then a loud, almost savage roar which seemed to rise from hundreds of human throats, "Up wid de Puck!" Still wondering greatly,

177

they at last entered the town, crowded now from end to end by parked cars and their occupants, whilst a continuous flow of mechanical music or announcements was poured out by a voice coming seemingly from the center of the square. This they avoided and the crowds of men and animals milling slowly round it, slipping down a side street to the circus where they found the second program about to begin. They knew where to find their costumes and, fortunate in meeting neither of the Salomons, they dressed quickly and then sought out Corky in his tent, ostensibly to borrow his comb for their wind-tangled hair, but in reality to hear from him if Otto had returned and what view had been taken of their own disappearance.

They found Curly there before them, he and Corky engaged in a conversation which was involving much shaking of heads and shrugging of shoulders. "And here they come," ended Corky, "all dressed up ready and looking as if butter wouldn't melt in their mouths!" And he burst into a guffaw.

"Has Otto come back?" they asked breathlessly, taking refuge in the oblique approach.

"No, he has *not*," Corky answered, "and I wouldn't be in your shoes either when you run into the Boss and Madame S. Had to fill up the time by coming in and doing some of his old conjuring tricks, he did, and when they heard they'd got the Boss instead of the act with the two clowns, he didn't half get booed. Cor, I'd give him a wide berth if I was you!"

At that moment a bell rang, indicating that the parade was about to begin.

"Here, get into your places quick before the Boss has time to notice," said Curly. "Come with us. You look fine! Just slip in there as if nothing had happened."

Madame Salomon was busy banging the big drum, the professor taking a last look at himself in the long glass. No one but the audience noticed as the twins came running and skipping in together.

"Ah, the lovely children!" they heard, "joined together, do you see? They do say that in Siam all the babies is born joined together the like of that and 'tis only in later life they comes unstuck. Ah, the pretty little fairies!" And a round of applause followed some of which, no doubt, the psychological pig and the mathematical horse quite rightly took to themselves but which to Dominic and Josephine seemed infinitely encouraging. At the end of the parade they managed to come to a halt as far as possible from where the professor was waiting to do his act with the pony and the row of numbers. They took refuge for some time in their own horse box, following the distant sounds of the circus until they heard the inscrutable Indian talking to his elephant, when they came out prepared to join in the waltz of "The Blue Danube." It was during the final tableau that Curly managed to murmur in Dominic's ear, "The Boss says, will ye go to his tent the very minute the show is over. He'll be waiting for you there."

"Bad luck, kiddoes! Don't let him see you're afraid of him," Corky whispered as, their faces visibly white in the absence of make-up but their heads held high, they approached the tent in which Authority sat. Dominic, who at school was not unacquainted with corporal punishment, thought of the professor's whip. Well, he shouldn't beat Josephine anyway. His eyes flashed as he stalked ahead of her into the tent and regarded the professor. "You sent for us, sir," he said.

The professor looked up and a scowl was beginning to spread over his face when a diversion occurred. Mr. Mac-Donagh, a whip in his hand, strode into the room wearing a scowl every bit as black as the professor's.

"Where's me daughter?" he roared.

"Your daughter?" echoed the professor, his scowl held as it were in suspension.

"Me daughter, sir," Mr. MacDonagh repeated. "She's gone, and I accuse you of hiding her here in your circus."

"But who is she, and why should she hide in my circus, of all places?" The professor was growing indignant.

"Because, by heaven, she loves your clown and has cried on me all the week to be allowed to meet him."

"But how can she love him if she has never met him?" The professor's indignation was giving place to bewilderment.

"Because, by the powers, she has met him when your circus was here last year, and since then she will hear nothing of the careful plans I am making for her future. And now she has gone, I'm telling you, and if ye don't hand her back this minute, I'll lay the horse-whip about ye till you're crying for pity on all fours!"

"One moment, sir, before you do anything you might regret." The professor eyed his own whip in the corner, the lash considerably longer and stronger even than that of the whip in Mr. MacDonagh's hand. "One moment. You say that your daughter has disappeared. At what hour did you notice her disappearance?"

"This morning she was gone," the other answered, glowering. "I needed her help in the bar and she was not there. But it was not till just now when I'm after finding her clothes gone and her box as well that I'm come to you to answer for her. And quick's the word, or I'll begin on you and no more said." He strode forward, the whip half-raised.

To do him justice, the professor did not blench or blink an eyelid. "Listen to me then," he said and pressed the wrathful man into a seat. "This morning my clown too was gone, and I thought nothing of it either till, needing him this afternoon for the act on which my circus hangs, I came upon his clown's dress hung up in his room and the rest of his belongings gone. Now I suggest that your daughter has enticed my clown away, and before we leave this town I shall be obliged regretfully to send you in a heavy bill for damages or by heaven your daughter shall return to me the best clown this circus has ever known."

In the course of the very heated argument that followed, Dominic and Josephine took the chance of obliterating themselves from the scene as noiselessly as possible. As they changed back into their own clothes, "So it wasn't," said Dominic, "such a very small world after all."

"No," answered his sister, "and I believe Orpine knew it was Otto she was going to meet at our party."

"As we were all from the same circus, I wouldn't put it past her," continued Dominic.

"Well, I'm glad we've made some one happy!" Josephine finished. Then they ran home and threw themselves breathlessly into the caravan.

"Oh, Kathleen," cried Dominic, and it was a cry from the heart. "Give us something to eat, please. We're nearly dying of hunger!"

"Now, the Lord love ye both! I thought never to see ye again!" Kathleen answered equably, beginning to stir a pot over the stove. "Here's your dinners I've kept back for ye, and you may as well have your teas with it. But tell me first, have ye found your goat? Not a sight of him? Ah, 'tis as I thought, for ye'll not find him in the mountains nor on the roads, nor anywhere in the wide world. But let ye look up in the heavens, and there ye'll see him set against the sky, and all the folks raising their voices to shout "Up wid de Puck!"

The children gaped, not certain whether or not to take this strange statement literally or as a flower of Kathleen's fancy. "It's the truth I'm telling ye. It's these eyes," said Kathleen, "have seen it!"

"*Seen* it?" echoed the children, more bewildered still.

"Ah, but what have I been telling ye all this while, and none to believe me? It's my sight been coming back to me! Many's the time I've set here and my bandage slipped, and looked on your goat the way I'd known him from a hundred others, just as I would yourselves from my own childer. And he's up there now, I'm telling ye, a crown of gold upon his head, a glory for all to behold! Swallow your victuals quick now, and go and see amn't I right!"

Hungry as they were, the children did not stay to carry out the first part of Kathleen's behest. Only waiting to drink their tea and clutching each a slice of raisin cake, they darted away and over the bridge to the market place. There were the two platforms, one above the other on a sort of Eiffel Tower-shaped erection, on the lower of which Tumaus and Larry were in the act of repeating their performance of "The Old Torn Petticoat" for which they had just been awarded first prize for the best double jig danced by children. Dominic and Josephine, however, had no eyes to spare for dancers when above their heads on a railed platform stood what was undoubtedly their goat.

"Yanadick!" they called together, their faces tilted skywards and by a miracle of sharp hearing, the goat heard them above the tumult of music and loud-speaker and answered them. One or two of the bystanders heard the faint cry from above and looked with curiosity at the children. "He's ours!" Josephine cried to one woman. "He was stolen from us whilst we were in the mountains!"

But the woman looked quickly away again. If the tinker

girl was trying to make out that the Puck was her own goat,
no doubt she was either mistaken or lying.

"How can we get him down?" Josephine turned frantically
to Dominic.

"Tonight," said Dominic, "we'll come back, when all
these people have gone home. They must have used pulleys
to hoist him up, so I suppose between us we could hoist him
down again."

"Oh, poor Yanadick!" cried Josephine in real distress.
"Just think how giddy he must be up there, and how
hungry!"

"Watch him," Dominic said. "I believe he's got something
to eat. I'm certain he was chewing the cud when we first saw
him. They couldn't leave him for two and a half days with
nothing to eat."

"Is it really as long as that?" cried Josephine, agonized,
"and aren't they afraid he'll jump off?"

"He'll not jump off," said a kindly-looking farmer who
was standing near them. "He'll be tied with good strong cords
by the four legs of him, and again round the horns. He'll be
safe so."

Dominic signed to Josephine to ask no more questions lest
the man's suspicions were aroused, and soon afterwards their
hunger led them back to the caravan where the twins were
showing their mother the trophy they had won, a silver-
mounted glass vase.

"She can see it! Our mam can see it!" the twins cried,
astonished and exulting. "Take your bandage off now,
Mam, and look at us all with your new eye!"

"No, not before the great doctor unbinds my eye himself,"
protested Kathleen. " 'Tis he has earned the reward of me
glad looks better than any. But here is one coming looking
for us, and a letter in his hand," she continued as a young
blue-eyed ragamuffin approached. "Take it from him, Dominic, if 'tis for us it's intended, and read what it is the words
does be saying."

" 'Tis from me sister," said the ragamuffin. "She gave it

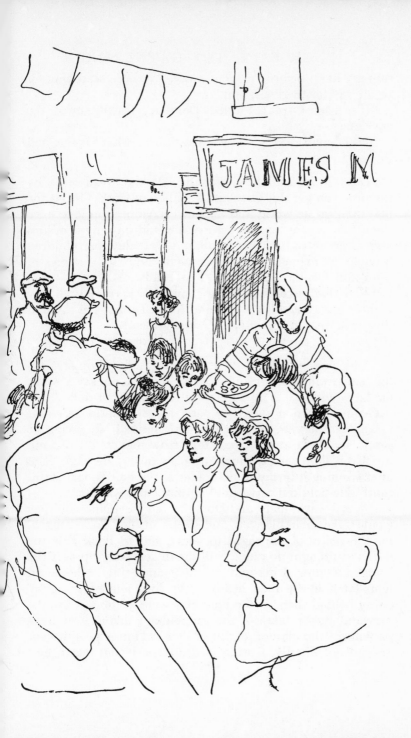

into my hand before she went away. I've been searching for ye all day for to give it you."

"It's from Orpine," cried Dominic, tearing open the envelope.

And of course every one wanted to hear what Orpine had to say.

"Dear Twins and Mrs. Hogan," Dominic read out. "By the time you get this Otto and I will be in Cork. Otto is the best man in the world and he and I have been in love since Puck Fair a year ago, but my dad would have none of him and so we were both very unhappy, but the dear children brought us to meet each other again and the blessings of Otto and Orpine will be on their heads for always. From Cork we shall take a passage to America where we shall stay with Otto's sister till we can find work. Do not tell my dad this or he may come after us. Your grateful

OTTO and ORPINE."

"And he would too," cried the ragamuffin, hopping delightedly from one foot to the other. "But I'll not say a word, for he would kill them surely and think it well done."

Orpine's brother stayed to eat a piece of raisin cake and to admire the vase and then he took himself off, saying he would see them at the circus tomorrow night. "But it's not my dad will give me the money for my ticket," he said. "I'm after winning it in the roulette tent at the Fair. Look you at that!" He held out a two-shilling piece and was gone.

It was a warm night and Dominic and Josephine said they would take their blankets and sleep outside. They listened for the noises of the night to abate, but to Puck Fair the darkness brought no quiet. Still the tinkers went up over the bridge for more drink and still they came singing home an hour later, to dip their heads in the river and begin again. Away behind them at the Fair they were keeping it up, the cars and motor bikes of the roundabout taking ever fresh passengers, the clamor of the mechanical music pealing ever on and on. Finally, fearing to drop asleep and leave their mission undone, the twins stole off together to the market place where at last humanity seemed to have gathered itself away to rest, save for the occasional step of a night reveller stumbling out of some pub and away down the street. Above their heads Yanadick and the stars; on the ground apparently none but themselves.

They crept up to the shadows of the scaffolding and, taking care to remain within their shelter, made their way to the center of the tower and had soon found the ropes and pulleys that controlled the elevation and descent of the goat's little platform. They eyed it with misgivings. "I wonder if it's as heavy as it looks," Dominic said dubiously and had just given one of the ropes a tentative little tug when a rough voice seemed suddenly to awaken from amongst the shadows and a heavy hand descended on Dominic's arm with an iron grip.

"Phwat are ye doing at all, tinker's brat?" cried the terrible voice. "Is it stealing our Puck ye are, and the luck of the town with him?"

"He isn't your Puck," Dominic answered back, equal in wrath. "He's ours, and someone has stolen him from us and put him up there, and we're going to get him down."

"You're going to get him down, you puny tinker, is it? Just you try to unloose they ropes, and he'll come down with such a run as will knock him to kingdom come and yourself as well. But you lie, for it's never a tinker's goat that he is, but a real mountainy one, and the best of his kind there's ever been."

"Tell me one thing," pleaded Dominic. "What are you going to do with him when Puck Fair is over?"

"Roast him and ate him too, I daresay," replied the furious man with a look of malevolence. "Now then, clear out of here right quick or I'll set the Gardai on to ye. Be off, the both of ye."

Burning now with rage and indignation, Dominic faced him, trying to think of an argument that would convince such a man of the rights of their claim. For a moment Josephine thought there would be a fight. Then Dominic, looking again at the heavy paraphernalia of ropes and pulleys, gave it up.

After all, as he said to Josephine as they slunk away home, it wouldn't help if they managed to kill Yanadick as they brought him down.

"So what are we going to do?" Josephine asked. "We can't leave him there to be roasted and eaten on Tuesday."

"We'll get Miley to help us, and we'll come back to-morrow night," Dominic answered, and the resolution in his voice gave her confidence again. "Some time that man must go to sleep!"

Josephine had an idea. "I know," she exclaimed, "I heard Corky say that the circus is giving its last two performances tomorrow. On Tuesday they're packing up and going on to Killarney. So tomorrow night we can ask the professor for our wages for the two days. How much do you think he will give us?"

Dominic pondered. "Only about five shillings a day each, the mean devil," he guessed. "That would make a pound altogether."

"Well, don't you think they'd sell us Yanadick for a pound? I've heard Nellie say that roast goat isn't very nice. I don't suppose the butcher would pay nearly as much as that for him."

"We could try," Dominic allowed, "but quite possibly the eating is part of some horrible old custom. Well, we'll see!"

By six o'clock on Monday night the second and last per-formance had ended and for the first time since their escapade of Sunday, Dominic and Josephine sought out the professor.

"If you please, sir," Dominic began brightly, "we've come for our wages."

"Your *what?*" cried the professor with a great show of anger. "And what do you think I'm going to give you for what you've done for me?"

"Well, sir, if you paid us each five shillings a day," Dominic answered, speaking very quickly as one not quite sure of his position, "that would make ten shillings each and one pound altogether."

"So you think I am going to give you a pound, do you, for your services to me and the circus?" said the professor, rising slowly to his feet. "Let me tell you that it is through you, miserable children, that I have lost Otto, the best clown I ever had and Madame Salomon's nephew to whom she was devoted—yes, devoted, I say! It was you, I hear, who planned this runaway act with the Orpine girl, a publican's daughter. You and they were seen, I hear, going off together for a drive the very night before their disappearance. And now, Madame and I don't even know where to look for them. Perhaps you can enlighten us?"

Dominic shut his mouth and shook his head.

"You can but you won't. Very well," continued the professor, his face beginning to turn a curious brick-red. "I'll show you what I'll give you for what you've done for us!" He leaned across and made a grab at Josephine, who was nearest to him.

Quick as thought and with his jaw set like a trap, Dominic rushed forward and ran between the professor's legs. The professor went down like a ninepin and Dominic, catching Josephine's hand as he sped past her, cried, "Away!" and they vanished like the wind. They had reached the far end of the fairground before they pulled up.

"So that's that!" uttered Dominic with what breath he had left.

"Thank goodness," gasped Josephine, "they're leaving tomorrow."

Near by stood an old patched tent which the twins had often seen though they had never troubled their heads to wonder what was inside. Now, in case the professor was still on their tracks, they slipped within and found it to be presided over by one of the hangers-on of the circus, an English gipsy of the name of Smith.

They stood and watched a small knot of men and boys who were bending over a large board with numbers painted on it in black and red and a small bowl round which a ping-pong ball was revolving. Occasionally one of them took a

sixpence out of his pocket and put it on the board; more rarely one of them put out his hand and took a couple of sixpences off the board. Whilst they watched, one lucky youth picked up a whole bunch of shillings and sixpences which were shovelled across to him, and walked whistling out of the tent.

Dominic became interested. Though all his shillings were gone, one of Sister Aloysia's sixpences remained in his pocket. He put it on the side of the odd numbers and it was on that side that the ball stopped. Then, whilst he was still hesitating as to his next move the ball was set spinning again and again it stopped on the odd numbers. This time two shillings were pushed towards him. So that was how Orpine's brother had

won his riches! Dominic watched the other players and saw
that some were putting their money on the red. He did the
same and again he won, and again his stake remained to
win once more. Now he had four shillings. He grew bolder
and put a sixpence straddling across a corner where four
numbers met. Trying to reckon what sum he would get if
this time he should be lucky, he looked up to find that he
had lost. This was the moment, he felt, for departure, but
he was careful to do it in the prescribed manner, both hands
in his pockets and whistling "The Blue Danube."

"How much have you got?" Josephine asked as they left
the tent.

"Only three and sixpence," Dominic admitted, "but somehow I felt as if I'd lose it all if I stayed."

They turned back into the town, past the shabby shops
and along the muddy pavements which bore traces of the
numbers of feet, human and animal, that had been visitors
to Puck Fair. At one shop Dominic lingered where the skin
of a stillborn calf was displayed, soft and dappled, side by
side with a fox's pelt, the beautiful brush combed out and
fluffy. Josephine wondered if Dominic intended to buy one
of these, so closely did he scrutinize them, but he passed on
to survey a tin of peaches in the next shop. "No," he announced then, "I shall wait till tomorrow. There are sure
to be some bargains on the last day of the Fair. Let's go back
to the caravan. We've got to make a plan with Miley, you
know, about tonight."

It was past midnight when three forms, of which two were
somewhat undersized and the third walked with the aid of a
pair of crutches, crossed the bridge and made their way up
through the town to the market place. The street was empty
except for a woman with a small baby tucked into her shawl,
who leaned over the figure of a young tinker, unconscious or
sleeping, his back propped against a railing where the road
crossed a gully. They tiptoed past her, but she did not
appear to notice them.

PUCK FAIR: THE GATHERING

The square was silent at last, the houses sleeping, but under the bright moon the scaffold stood out, black in the silver light; at its highest pinnacle a figure so still that it might have been sculpted in ebony, with beard and silver-bright horns. They wondered if he were asleep: if he had seen them come?

One thing was certain in the clear moonlight. There was no watcher, no human guardian's form at the foot of the scaffold. But for all that their approach was made with the utmost caution, stealthily and in complete silence. They looked again at the sculptured form, but in the brief moment something had changed in the goat's posture. There was no doubt now that he was wide awake, his ears pricked forward, listening intently to a sound that had not reached them. It was Miley who heard it first. " 'Tis the Green-coated Boy!" he whispered, "his own song that he's singing."

Now the children heard it too, far away though it was:

> *To the lakes of delight that no storm may curl*
> *Where the teeth are as pearl, the eyes as sloes,*
> *Which alight, whenever they choose to seek,*
> *On the bloom of a cheek, where the foxglove glows.*

"What shall we do?" Josephine whispered urgently to Miley.

"Do? Nothing at all. 'Tis that one will do all the doing. Only sit quiet and he'll be here."

Now in the direction where the voice had been there was a low murmuring as though a town were awaking. The song sounded again, but from the direction of the bridge it seemed, and much nearer.

"He can do that with his voice," Miley murmured. "Throw it here and throw it there as 'twere an echo. I'll lay it's nowhere near the bridge he is at all."

There was a shout. "It's they children again! It's no good they're up to." They recognized the voice and heard a patter of feet running away towards the bridge. The next moment the Boy stood by their side.

"Quick, Miley! I know the way. Let you take that rope and I this. Josephine and Dominic, stand you each beside one of us and add your weight to ours. Now, hold you with all your might. Steady it is!"

Dominic and Josephine added every ounce they had to the rope and between the four of them there was just enough weight. Slowly they passed the rope upwards hand over hand till at last the floor of Yanadick's platform was seen descending over their heads. As soon as it bumped to earth the Boy whipped out a knife and a piece of cord. "Fasten this lead around his neck, Dominic," said he. "Josephine, pull the cords asunder as fast as I cut them—now! Ah, the poor beast, it's stiff he is and no marvel in it!"

Yanadick, half-dazed but free, stood in their midst. "Now, follow me quick," said the Boy and with the goat close behind disappeared down a narrow alley leading in the direction of the mountains. Dominic and Josephine, clutching his lead, were dragged along behind whilst Miley, on his crutches, kept pace by the wall. In a few moments their feet were soundless on the soft turf. Keeping still in the shadow of the town walls till they were certain of being unobserved, they crossed the upper road and made a detour back towards the caravan.

"Tether him where he was before," said the Green-coated Boy hurriedly. "Nobody knew 'twas there he came from and he wandering the hills. He's safe now—your own again!"

They turned to thank him but already he had vanished. A few minutes later they heard his song on the road to the mountains. At the same moment there was a roar of angry voices from the square. The three looked at each other awestruck. "They've found him gone!" said Miley.

CHAPTER XX

Puck Fair: The Scattering

"Where are you going?" Josephine asked Dominic next morning.

"Going shopping; remember that three and six?"

"What are you going to buy?"

"Come with me and you'll see!"

Every one was leaving. First one caravan and then another pulled out, crossed the bridge and climbed up through the square to the main road beyond. Soon theirs would be gone too. Miley had urged Kathleen to have everything ready to break camp as early as possible on this day—the day of the Scattering. Kathleen had promised, and then there had been a hitch. An axle pin was missing which had certainly been in its place on the day of their arrival. It looked very much as though on the night of the dancing in the glen someone in need of an axle pin had come unawares and helped himself. Now Miley had gone to the forge to have a new one made, but the forge was fully occupied fitting travellers' horses with shoes. Miley was told he must wait his turn.

It was soon after this news came that Dominic, who had been showing signs of acute anxiety, decided to go shopping. He hurried Josephine past the manifold sights of a whole townsfolk of caravans limbering up and getting ready for the road.

Two members of the Garda were standing at the entrance

to the barracks which looked up the square. They seemed to be regarding the empty scaffold and speculating on the fate of the Puck when Josephine noticed that the eyes of the elder of the two had come to rest upon herself and Dominic. Their heads moved towards each other as though they were sharing in some confidence.

"Dominic," she said a moment later. "Did you notice anything about those two Gardai?"

"Yes," Dominic answered. "They seemed to be talking about us."

"I . . . I wonder what they were saying?" Josephine went on rather faintly as he said nothing further.

"So do I!" Dominic answered grimly. "We'll go back another way."

They arrived at the shop where the evening before they had seen the fox's pelt and the skin of the stillborn calf displayed. Dominic entered and stood looking at each in turn.

"How much is this one?" he asked, handling the calf-skin.

"Ten shillings and no less," replied the old vendor, who might have been poor relation to a vet. "'Tis a pedigree Ayrshire from Major Fogarty's herd. The price of the other's the same, and a better brush ye'll never see!"

"I'll give you three and six for the two," said Dominic, holding out the money. "It's all I've got."

The old man looked at it and pondered deeply. "Aw, take the both of them," he said suddenly. "Take care ye don't get the moth mixed up in it!" he advised over his shoulder as Dominic made off with the skins.

"I'll take care," Dominic promised.

They walked all round the square so as not to pass the barracks. Back at the caravan Dominic asked Kathleen for any odd bits of string she might have handy. With a fistful of miscellaneous tapes and broken bootlaces, he made his way across to Yanadick, followed by Josephine.

"Now boy, we've got you a new coat. You're going to wear a disguise," he told the goat.

Yanadick, who at first had seemed both exhausted and

ravenous, was now beginning to act more like himself. He reared up as Dominic approached with the fox's pelt and made a great show of butting at it with his horns.

"No, this isn't a game," Dominic told him. "It's dead earnest. You're still in time to be roasted and eaten, remember!"

Josephine, seeing at last where all this was leading, helped Dominic to find eight of the strongest bootlaces in Kathleen's collection and attach them firmly to the eight legs of fox and calf. "Now you must scratch his head," Dominic ordered, "whilst I tie them round his chest and tummy. We'll have the fox first, I think."

A few minutes later Yanadick stood before them, a fox's brush ornamenting his hind quarters and a pedigree Ayrshire's pelt covering his body. Never had the goat looked more unlovely. It was plain that he resented his disguise deeply, and his antics, as he skipped and turned himself about trying to tear at the horrid garments with his teeth, had the children laughing heartily in spite of the anxiety of the moment, and fetched Kathleen out from the caravan to see what was afoot.

But suddenly they were aware of other laughter mingling with their own. Two men of the Gardai laughed too, the very same that the children had seen earlier that morning, and here they stood beside the caravan watching Yanadick's antics with every appearance of the deepest enjoyment.

The children gazed at them speechless, the springs of all laughter suddenly run dry, but the Gardai suffered from no such inhibitions. The elder man carried a large notebook with which he now advanced upon Dominic and Josephine. They realized they were about to be cross-questioned.

"Name of?" he inquired of Josephine. Her eye sought Dominic's questioningly. "Better tell them," he answered. "We don't want to get the Hogans into trouble."

So they told everything the Gardai wanted to know; their names, their ages and the date of their birth.

"Twins, are ye?" said the younger one. "Ye put me in

mind of another pair of twins I've seen recently, but they were Salomon's Siamese Twins from the circus, so I must have been mistook."

"But Salomon's circus is after leaving the town," said the older man. "Do ye not travel with them any more?"

"No," answered Dominic with reserve. "We . . . we've had a row."

The elder man laughed. "Ye're none the worse for that, I daresay," he said. "They're quare people, the circus folk. And this goat? Ye're having quite a game with him, I can see. Does he belong to you?"

"Yes, sir, he *does*!" The explosive force of Dominic's assertion made the Garda stare. "Well," he said, pocketing his notebook, "we'll be seeing you again I daresay. You don't look like being ready to start yet." And the two men took their leave.

"I didn't care for those men at all," said Kathleen as soon as they were out of earshot, "and the cunning looks on their faces as though ye couldn't tell them anything that they hadn't heard already. And I, who have always been on the side of the Law! 'Tis for the goat they have come surely, and I fear they may wrench him from ye yet."

"Do you think they'll put us in prison?" asked Josephine, her voice fearful.

"The Holy Saints forbid!" answered Kathleen and crossed herself. "Run quickly now, Dominic, to the forge where Miley waits and bid him bring me any piece of machinery that will hould a wheel together. We must begone, tell him, and make no more delay. Come back then and tell me what he answers."

Dominic didn't need bidding twice. He was off and away and back again whilst the others were still wondering how far he had gone upon the road.

"The smith was working on the pin whilst I was there," he told them. "It can't be long now."

But still Miley unaccountably delayed. The church clock struck one; somewhere a train came in, whistled and departed. Only one other van now remained, that of their nearest neighbors on the camping-ground with whom they were friendly.

"Here's someone coming!" cried Josephine at last, and they realized then how intolerable had been the suspense. But it was not Miley but the Gardai who came.

"Quick, Josephine, into that cart!" cried Dominic, and together they had hurtled into the neighbor's spare cart, which was empty and covered by a tarpaulin, before the Gardai had come round the corner of the caravan.

At first the thumping of their hearts was the only sound they heard. "But where are the children?" they heard one of the men ask.

Her eye to a chink in the tarpaulin, Josephine saw then that two other figures had appeared behind the Gardai. One look at them and she was out of the cart, followed by Dominic, and in their arms.

"Mummy, Daddy!" they cried together, and in that moment all the pressing cares and fears of the last three days dissolved away. "Mummy, Daddy, how did you get here?"

"*You* are nice ones to ask that," said their father, "when every one has been telling us you were drowned!"

"But we never believed it," cried their mother, "not till they found your bodies. And now we've found you instead."

"But why did they think we were drowned?" Dominic asked, trying to sort things out.

"Because one of Mrs. Markham's sons had seen you start off in a canoe two days after the Major's sale and was ready to swear it was the same canoe that was found in a backwater of the Shannon a week later," their father explained.

"And tied on to the canoe," their mother added, "was a queer sort of Eastern doll that Nellie was sure Josephine had brought home from the sale."

"And is she still there?" cried Josephine, very elated.

"She's waiting for you at home," her mother assured her.

The children pondered again. "But didn't you get our postcards from Cashel?" Dominic asked. The parents shook their heads. "I expect they came after we'd left," said their mother. "We flew home the moment we got Uncle Theo's cable saying you were gone. Ever since there have been photographs of you posted up in all the barracks in Ireland."

"And little I thought," said the younger Garda, tiring of being an audience in a scene in which he had played so important a part, "little I thought when I treated the sergeant here to a ticket for Salomon's circus that Salomon's Siamese Twins could be the very ones as had had all Ireland guessing these six weeks and more. And they that have come unstuck, I'm thinking, since the day that the circus was over!"

The children laughed. "Oh, that was almost the last of all our adventures," Dominic explained to their parents. "Puck Fair was to be the last of all, and then Kathleen and her twins and Miley were going to bring us home again in their caravan. This is Kathleen," he said, presenting them. "Those are our fellow-twins, Larry and Tumaus, the champion step-dancers of Puck Fair"—the Hogan twins came shyly forward—"and oh, here's Miley at last with the axle pin!"

Miley indeed it was who entered running, if ever a pair of crutches could be said to run, the axle pin hanging round his neck.

"Holy Saints, the Gardai!" he cried in dismay.

"It doesn't matter now, Miley," said Josephine. "These are our parents come to thank you and Kathleen for taking such good care of us all this long time."

And for some time nothing more was said on any other subject, whilst Kathleen and Miley protested that the dear children had been as the light of their eyes and the works of their hands. "Indeed," said Kathleen, "we'll keep them for ye gladly till your next leave, and their uncle sparing them."

The children's mother laughed happily. "But this *is* our next leave," she said, "and after this we don't go back again. There's Home Rule in the Gold Coast now and they don't need us any more."

"But I've been given a new job as Queen's Messenger," their father added, "so we'll be living at home now."

"And we'll never leave you again," their mother added.

"But what, may I ask, is this animal?" asked their father, his eye suddenly arrested by Yanadick, with his fox's brush and his dappled jacket, "and what part does he play in the story?"

"Yes, indeed," the sergeant broke in, "and there is one that has been in the public eye himself, unless I'm much mistaken!" And he gave the twins a shrewd look.

But by the time they had finished telling the saga that began with the little white goat and ended at Puck Fair, the day was considerably older and, Dominic and Josephine completely cleared of the charge of Puck-stealing, the Gardai had returned to their barracks.

"And the Green-coated Boy?" their mother said. "How are we ever to find so mysterious a person and thank him too for his part in all this?"

"How are we to find him?" Josephine echoed. "Oh, some fine day in spring we shall hear his pipes playing and he'll suddenly be there saying, "Where's that little kid you promised me?"